To Gloria
Kortmeyer.
Best wishes
Constance C. Greene

ISABELLE
and
Little Orphan Frannie

ISABELLE
and
Little Orphan
Frannie

BY CONSTANCE C. GREENE

VIKING KESTREL

VIKING KESTREL
Published by the Penguin Group
Viking Penguin Inc., 40 West 23rd Street, New York, New York 10010, U.S.A.
Penguin Books Ltd, 27 Wrights Lane, London W8 5TZ England
Penguin Books Australia Ltd, Ringwood, Victoria, Australia
Penguin Books Canada Ltd, 2801 John Street, Markham, Ontario, Canada L3R 1B4
Penguin Books (N.Z.) Ltd, 182–190 Wairau Road, Auckland 10, New Zealand

Penguin Books Ltd, Registered Offices: Harmondsworth, Middlesex, England

First published in 1988 by Viking Penguin Inc.
Published simultaneously in Canada

Library of Congress Cataloging in Publication Data
Greene, Constance C.   Isabelle and little orphan Frannie / by Constance C. Greene;
illustrated by Diane deGroat.   p. cm.
Summary: When Isabelle discovers her new protégée can't read, she
acquires an unwilling and possibly unteachable pupil.
ISBN 0-670-82266-3
[1. Reading—Fiction.]   I. De Groat, Diane, ill.   II. Title.
PZ7.G8287In   1988   [Fic]—dc19   87-35558

Printed in the United States of America by Arcata Graphics, Fairfield, Pennsylvania
Set in Aster.

1   2   3   4   5   92   91   90   89   88

*To all the Frannies out there
this book is for you.*

ISABELLE
and
Little Orphan Frannie

ONE

"Can I come in?"

The voice came from outside. Isabelle scooped a fingerful of peanut butter from the jar and held it aloft, listening. A distant baby squalled. A car with a bum muffler rattled past. Some show-off teenagers shouted insults and turned up the volume on their blaster, scattering bits of loud music like feathers on the wind.

"Who are you?" Isabelle asked.

"I'm Frannie," the voice answered.

"I don't know any Frannie," Isabelle said, and scuttled, crablike, across the floor, peering out to see what Frannie looked like.

A skinny girl with spiky pale hair and wearing a skirt that brushed the tops of her basketball sneakers stood on the path. She wore a huge T-shirt that said "BABY INSIDE," with an arrow pointing to her flat stomach. It was one of those T-shirts pregnant people wore, and Isabelle would've loved one. She imagined her mother's face if she appeared suddenly, wearing one of those shirts. Preferably when one of her mother's friends was there for a visit. Lovely, lovely. Every time Isabelle's mother saw someone wearing one of those shirts, she tch-tched and said, "In my day people didn't advertise their condition."

"Your day is long gone, Mom," Isabelle liked to reply.

"That's what you think," Isabelle's mother was apt to reply back.

"Can I come in?" Frannie asked a second time.

"Why not?" Isabelle said, and swung open the door. Frannie scooted inside and stood, tapping her foot, checking out everything in sight.

"I thought perhaps you might have a little something for me to eat," she said, cool as a cucumber.

Isabelle held out her finger coated with peanut butter in a gesture of friendship, and slowly, as delicate as a cat, Frannie licked the peanut butter from it.

"That tickles," Isabelle said.

"How about a cracker?" Frannie said.

4

"Frannie wants a cracker," Isabelle parroted, and handed over a box of saltines.

Frannie frowned. "Not that kind," she said.

"Take it or leave it, kid. My mother says if you're really hungry, you'll eat anything." Reluctantly Frannie helped herself to a saltine.

Fresh from swim practice and smelling strongly of chlorine from the Y pool, Philip crashed into the kitchen.

"Foo!" Isabelle held her nose. "You stink."

"Stand back, turd. I need nourishment before I do my paper route." Philip grabbed the box of saltines from Frannie and stuffed a handful into his mouth, sending up a spray of crumbs.

"Who's the weird-looking chick?" he said.

"Her name's Frannie," Isabelle replied.

"I'm not weird-looking," said Frannie. "You got any bananas?"

"She looks a little bit skeevy to me," said Philip. "Where'd she come from?"

"The upper reaches of the atmosphere," said Isabelle, smiling mysteriously.

"Just over there," and Frannie waved an arm.

"I didn't know the circus was in town." Philip laughed hugely, as if he'd said something funny. "I know." He pointed to Frannie. "You're a clown. Or maybe a lion tamer. That's it, a lion tamer. Am I right?"

Undisturbed, Frannie smiled a snaggle-toothed smile.

5

"I'm a norphan," she said.

"A what?"

"A norphan," she repeated.

"What's a norphan?" Isabelle asked.

"What!" Philip's eyes bugged out in astonishment. "You never heard of a norphan? Any wonko knows what a norphan is." He proceeded to make himself a three-decker Dagwood special: cheese, salami, and tomato. Frannie watched with interest.

"What's that?" she said.

"This? This here is fuel for the mighty engine," and Philip thumped his chest so hard he almost landed on the floor. He was so full of himself Isabelle knew he must've won today. Whenever he came in first in the butterfly, his speciality, he practically floated over the treetops, like Mary Poppins coming in for a landing.

"Can I have one?" Frannie asked, eyeing the sandwich.

"Help yourself." Philip shoved the bread and fixings toward her. "I'm late." He checked his new digital watch, bought with money saved from his paper route. You'd think he was the first person on planet Earth to own a digital watch, Isabelle thought sourly.

"Earth to Philip, vamoose," she said, but he was already gone.

"Who's that?" Frannie asked.

"Philip. He's my brother. He's thirteen. It's a very bad age, thirteen. My father says he's feeling his oats. All I know is, he's very, very obnoxious."

Frannie spread the mayo carefully, so it reached the crusts but didn't ooze over the sides.

"What's a norphan?" Isabelle said.

After some thought, Frannie laid a slice of cheese carefully over the mayo. "A norphan is a person that doesn't have a father. That's what a norphan is."

"Oh," said Isabelle, light breaking. "You mean an orphan."

"That's what I said, isn't it?" Frannie took a careful bite. "That's just what I said. A norphan."

TWO

"So then"—*Frannie ran her tongue around her mouth*
slowly, making sure no stray crumb had escaped her—
"My old daddy died and my mom went looking for a
new one. She traded in her Chevy for a Caddy and
put a bumper sticker on it that says, 'If You're Rich,
I'm Single,' then she got her eyebrows plucked and
her hair permed and dropped about ten pounds and
took off. Now we're living with Aunt Ruth. Well"—
Frannie lifted both hands, palms up—"she's not *really*
our aunt, you see, but she wants us to call her that.

What's it to me if she is or isn't? I could care less."

"How can you be an orphan if you've got a mother?" Isabelle asked, wondering if Frannie was telling the truth or had borrowed her material from a new soap opera.

"That's all right." Frannie had all the answers, apparently. "If your daddy dies, you're still a norphan. That's what my mom said. Can I use the facilities, please?"

"Facilities?"

"The bathroom." Frannie pursed her lips. "Aunt Ruth says ladies call it the facilities if they have any class."

Isabelle led Frannie to the bathroom. "Don't forget to jiggle the handle after you flush. It'll run if you don't jiggle."

When Frannie returned, she said, "I jiggled, but it didn't do any good."

"Isabelle, I told you to jiggle the handle, didn't I?" Isabelle's mother appeared and plunked down a huge bag of groceries. "Hello, I'm Isabelle's mother," she said, noticing Frannie. "Who are you?"

"This is Frannie," Isabelle said. "She's an orphan."

"A what?" said Isabelle's mother, half in, half out of the refrigerator.

"A norphan," Frannie said complacently.

"Her old daddy died," Isabelle explained," and her mom's out looking for a new one."

Isabelle's mother almost dropped a dozen eggs. Too

9

bad, Isabelle thought. She longed to take off her Adidas and walk barefoot through all those yolks and whites, letting them squish between her toes.

"Poor little thing." Isabelle's mother's face crumpled, as if she might cry. "I'm so sorry. Poor child. Are you staying with relatives then, Frannie? Someone who looks out for you?"

"Well, my Aunt Ruth works very hard. When she comes home, she just tosses hot dogs into the microwave. Those things get nuked so fast it makes your head spin. We eat nuked hot dogs almost every night," Frannie said.

"Well, then, you must come and have supper with us some night."

"I can't stay tonight," Frannie said. "It's pancake night."

"Pancake night?" Isabelle said. "I thought people only ate pancakes for breakfast."

"Aunt Ruth works at the Pancake Hut, and they give her all their leftovers. So she brings 'em home and nukes 'em in the microwave. We have blueberry ones and strawberry ones and all kinds."

"Oh, my." Isabelle's mother shook her head, thinking, no doubt, that that was hardly a balanced diet for a child.

This orphan business was all right, Isabelle thought, narrowly watching her mother. Right off the bat she's asking a total stranger over for supper. How come? We don't even *know* Frannie, for Pete's sake.

"Mom." Isabelle turned to her mother. "If you and Daddy died, would I be a whole orphan?"

"A little tact is in order, Isabelle," her mother hissed.

"Anyway, it's just as well she can't stay tonight." Isabelle stood on her head, showing off. "Oh, how I love the library! I have to go to the library tonight to get out some books." Her voice had a grand hollow ring when she talked standing on her head, she thought.

"Since when?" asked Isabelle's mother. "It's news to me."

"I just love books!" Isabelle crooned, flipping over and lying on her back on the kitchen floor. "I just love to read. I read books all the time. Do you like to read?" she asked Frannie.

"How many books did you read?" Frannie said.

Isabelle closed her eyes and pretended to count. "I'd say about a thousand. Give or take."

"Yeah, give or take quite a few." Her mother's voice floated over her head like a hot air balloon. "Isabelle, garbage, please."

"Why can't Philip do it?" Isabelle whined. "He's a boy. Boys are supposed to carry out the garbage. He always gets out of doing stuff like that."

"If you please." Her mother stood over her, brandishing a bulging plastic bag as if it were a sword.

"Yech," Isabelle said.

"Right away, please." The garbage bag seemed to swell, and Isabelle imagined it full of moving things: spiders, ants, and tiny, well-fed grubs.

11

As Isabelle and Frannie went out, Frannie said, "Your mother is a very lovely person," in a penetrating voice.

"She's not so much," Isabelle mumbled.

"I think she's truly a super person," Frannie continued in an even louder voice. "You are lucky to have such a super lovely person for a mother."

Isabelle saw her mother's shadow lingering by the back door, taking it all in. Isabelle's mother was known for her excellent hearing. She was always losing her glasses, but her ears were great. Just ask her.

"Well," said Isabelle in her hog-calling voice, "she's not *really* my mother."

"She's not?" Frannie said, surprised.

"Nope." Isabelle dumped the garbage bag into the can and put the top on tight. "She's really my grandmother, you see." The shadow gasped, and Isabelle grinned.

"Your grandmother!" Frannie exclaimed. "She certainly doesn't *look* that old."

"Yeah, well." Isabelle smiled as she took a couple of swipes at Frannie's head with her friendship ring. "She just got her face lifted."

THREE

Right after the six o'clock news, Herbie showed up, look-ing for a fight. Acting as if nothing had happened. Acting as if he hadn't chosen Chauncey Lapidus to be his right-hand man when he was elected art editor of the *Bee* to fill Sally Smith's shoes when Sally moved away. Isabelle still had hurt feelings that Herbie hadn't chosen her, Isabelle, to do the job.

"Let's tangle, Iz," Herbie sang out, taking his box-er's stance. "I got a couple new moves I want to try. A couple things guaranteed to send you sky-high. Come on out."

"Go soak your head, Herb," Isabelle said. "Go pick a fight with Chauncey, why doncha? You and him are such big buddies. Go knock his socks off." Sarcasm coated her tongue and made it thick in her mouth.

"Gimme a break," Herbie whined. "What'd I do to you? What's your beef? Why would I want to go pick a fight with Chauncey anyway? That'd be like punching a bag full of marshmallows."

Isabelle's face remained stony. "Take off, Herb," she told him. "You and me have had it. We've come to the end of the road."

"What's your prob? I didn't do nothing. I'm your best pal." In his agitation, Herbie pushed his face against the screen. "We been pals ever since nursery school. Now you're dumping on me. It ain't fair," he wailed.

"Fair's fair," Isabelle said coldly. But it was true. They had been best pals ever since Miss Ginny's nursery school, when they'd discovered they both liked to fight. They'd been fighting ever since, sometimes at her house, sometimes at his. Miss Ginny had threatened to throw them both out if they didn't stop. They were giving her school a bad name, she said.

And now they were in fifth grade.

"You and me go back a long way, Iz," said Herbie dolefully.

Herbie began jumping up and down, as he always did when he got excited. Isabelle loved it when Herbie did that.

14

"Chauncey forced me!" Herbie cried. "I wanted you, but Chauncey said he was responsible for my land-slide so I had to make him my right-hand man. He said that was the rule. I tell you, Iz"—Herbie shook his head and shot her a somber look—"it was a dark and stormy night when I landed that spot. I don't even know what an art editor *does*, for Pete's sake!"

"I buy that, Herb. I don't either," Isabelle admitted. "Who does? I don't think even Sally Smith knew, and she was a star. Sally faked it a lot."

"So now Chauncey's organizing a campaign to make himself art editor of the *Bee*," Herbie said. "And who do you think's gonna be his right-hand man?"

"Beats me," Isabelle said. "Who?"

"Mary Eliza Shook, that's who! She already gave Chauncey the word. Put me in office, she said, or else. You got Mary Eliza for an enemy, you don't need anybody else, right?"

"Yeah! Yeah!" Isabelle cried. To celebrate, she decked Herbie with one well-aimed punch to the nose. As he hit the dirt, blood started to flow.

"I'm getting weaker by the minute," Herbie gasped, catching the drops of blood in his cupped hand. "One, two, three," he droned. "If I die, Iz, you can have my ten-speed bike and my Havahart trap."

Isabelle had had her eye on that Havahart trap for a long time. With it, she had high hopes of catching a muskrat or a raccoon or even a skunk. "Stay right there," she said and raced inside. When she got back, clutching a paper cup full of ice cubes, Herbie was stretched flat out, pale and still, studying the sky. She knelt and pushed an ice cube up each of Herbie's nostrils.

Whereupon Herbie let out a bloodcurdling war whoop and leaped upon Isabelle as if he'd been fired from a cannon.

"You turkey! You toad! You rat cheat!" Isabelle hollered as she fell.

With one foot firmly on her stomach, Herbie felt like king of the hill. His nose had stopped bleeding, and he was, for the moment, victorious.

"Next time you get a nosebleed, I'm gonna sit there and watch," Isabelle stormed. "Wait and see. No tourniquet, no nothing, I'm just letting you drip until there's no more to drip. You'll be the original drip-dry kid. Just rinse you out and hang you up and, boy, will you be pale! You'll look like a ghost. Ghosts don't have any blood, you know. And when Dracula takes a peek at you, he'll say phooey, because it won't be worth his while to suck your blood out of you because it's all gone. What a mess."

Unmoved by all this, Herbie pressed his foot down harder and said, "Okay, if that's the way you feel, I'm taking back my ten-speed and my Havahart."

"So you're an Indian giver and a cheat and a toad and all the rest." Isabelle looked past Herbie and said, "Oh, hi, how are you, little orphan Frannie. Meet Herbie, the biggest creep on the block. Frannie's old daddy

16

died, Herb, and her mom's out looking for a new one." Isabelle spoke in her best hostess manner as she performed introductions.

Herbie turned to see who was there. No one. In the flick of an eye Isabelle seized the advantage and succeeded in flipping Herbie off her and down to the ground. Once there, she pounded Herbie's head into the dirt.

"I'm bleeding, I'm bleeding!" Herbie cried. "No fair using feet. That's cheating."

"Look who's talking."

"Isabelle! Time!" Her mother's voice rang out.

"Coming!" Isabelle gave Herbie's head one last thump and took off at a high rate of speed for home.

Herbie got to his feet, hitched up his trousers and, muttering to himself, headed for home. His mother would have a fit when she saw the blood all over his shirt. So who cared. His mother had lots of fits. She always recovered.

And after supper Isabelle went to her room and wrote on her blackboard in big letters: "HERBIE IS A WEASEL AND A TOAD AND A CHEAT."

She stood back to see how it looked. Then she added: "AND A TURKEY."

Then, after further scrutiny, she wrote in very small letters: "i have read 43 books."

That looked good, if not exactly the case.

She went back to the blackboard, crossed out the

"43" and put in its place "½" and erased the "s" on "books" so it read right.

"At least I tell the truth," Isabelle announced to the empty room. "That's more than some people I know."

FOUR

"I got a postcard from Sally Smith," said Jane Malone next morning before the bell rang. "She loves her new school. She's made two new friends already. Her new teacher is nice, she says, but not as nice as Mrs. Esposito."

"I probably got one too," Isabelle said. "I forgot to check the mail. Sally said she was going to write me every day. Maybe she lost my address. I wrote it on a teeny little piece of paper."

She felt a sharp stab of pain. Maybe Sally Smith

had written to everybody except her. Sally was her friend. Maybe she'd run out of stamps. Maybe she had writer's cramp from writing postcards to everyone in town except Isabelle.

"Hello there." Quick as a wink, Mary Eliza shot her arm through Isabelle's and held her in her iron grip.

"Guess what?" Before Mary Eliza opened her big bazoo, Isabelle knew what she was going to say.

"I got a postcard from Sally Smith." Mary Eliza said it. "She has two cute boys on her new block. One of them's in her class. She cried for two whole days, she was so homesick. But now she likes her new house and her new school and the two cute boys. Isn't that too much?" Mary Eliza relaxed her grip for a second and Isabelle took off. If Chauncey told her that he got a postcard from Sally Smith, she thought she might throw up.

"Hey, Isabelle! How ya doing?" Guy Gibbs yelled.

"Hi, Guy," Isabelle said. "How's it going?" She could tell from looking at him that Guy was doing fine. His face was shiny with happiness, and he swung his arms when he walked, like a big shot. Anyone could see he was a new man.

"Pretty good," said Guy. "My friend Bernie and me are raising worms. We expect a bumper crop. We're opening a stand in Bernie's front yard this summer. Our worms are guaranteed first class. If you don't catch anything with one of our worms, you get your money back," Guy said, very serious. "Purchase one

20

of our worms and you can't go wrong." Guy reeled off his sales pitch without a hitch.

"What if all I catch with one of your worms is a beat-up tire or somebody's underwear or something?" Isabelle said. "Do I get my money back then too?"

"Bernie and me will have to talk it over then, I guess," Guy said.

"Fishing's boring," Isabelle said. "All you do is sit there and wait for a bite. My father took me once and never again! He said I was too itchy to be a fisherman and he's right. Good luck, Guy, on your worms."

"Thanks," Guy said. "Me and Bernie plan to clean up. See ya," and he set off, arms swinging to beat the band.

"I don't care if it *is* spring," Mrs. Esposito was saying as Isabelle skidded into her seat. "I want and expect to see a change in behavior in this class. There's entirely too much horsing around. Drastic action will be taken if it continues. No recess, no free periods, extra homework." People rustled in their seats and let out little groans. When Mrs. Esposito went on the war path, watch out.

"Now please listen carefully to tomorrow's English assignment. I want you to . . ."

A sudden loud pop came from Herbie's desk. He'd blown a super duper bubble and it had burst. All over his face. He was covered with bubble gum from his eyebrows to his chin. He looked so funny the class roared. Even the corners of Mrs. Esposito's mouth turned up for an instant.

"Go for it, Herb!" Isabelle yelled.

"Herbie, go to the boys' room and get rid of that stuff. Wash your face. Scrape it off it you have to. And if I catch you chewing gum in class one more time, you go straight to the principal's office."

Isabelle ran her finger across her throat and said in a loud voice, "She means it's curtains for you, Herb."

"That's enough!" Mrs. Esposito snapped. "That's yet another example of the kind of behavior I meant, the kind I will not tolerate. One more peep out of you, Isabelle, and you go the same route. Now sit down and be quiet."

Isabelle sat.

Mrs. Esposito cleared her throat.

"One more thing, class, before I give you the assignment." Her voice was calmer now.

"I want to read you a postcard I got from Sally Smith."

"Oh, no!" Isabelle cried, slapping herself on the forehead. "I can't stand it! I positively, absolutely cannot stand it."

Mrs. Esposito waited.

"Are you finished, Isabelle?" she said at last.

"Yes, sir," said Isabelle.

FIVE

"I'm painting my guest room pale blue," said Mrs. Stern. "Did you know pale blue wards off evil spirits?" she asked, smiling so Isabelle would know she was only fooling around.

"Have you got any evil spirits?" Isabelle asked excitedly. She had always longed to see some evil spirits, not necessarily up close, though.

"It's just an old superstition," Mrs. Stern said. "Down South they paint the trim on doors and windows pale blue because it's supposed to ward off evil spirits.

Don't ask me why, but I rather like the idea. I wouldn't know an evil spirit if I fell over it."

"Me either," Isabelle agreed. "Maybe it'd look like Mary Eliza Shook. I wouldn't be surprised to find out Mary Eliza Shook was queen of the evil spirit club. Why not paint the guest room the same color as your front door? That's a neat color, that bright red. It's very peppy and sparkly. You can't ignore that color even if you try."

"Well, it's one thing to have a front door that color and quite another to paint a guest room bright red. It might give your guests jangly nerves, and that would never do." Mrs. Stern gave Isabelle's shoulder a friendly pat. Already Isabelle felt better. Mrs. Stern was a cheerer upper, and Isabelle felt in need of cheering up. It had been a bad day.

"Are you having guests?" Isabelle asked.

Mrs. Stern bustled about, getting down the marshmallows and the Oreos. Oreos always cheered *her* up, Isabelle thought, getting her teeth ready for that first bite.

"Yes, I am," Mrs. Stern said. "An old friend is coming to stay. I want the room to look nice. He'll stay for a week, maybe longer."

"Oh, it's a boy, then," Isabelle said.

"A man, yes," Mrs. Stern said, blushing. Isabelle almost fell over in surprise. She didn't know old people knew how to blush. She thought only kids blushed, mostly when they did something embarrassing.

"I told you about him, Isabelle. His sister was my dear old friend, and she left me a ring when she died, and he brought it to me."

"Do you like him?"

"One marshmallow or two?" Mrs. Stern dropped two marshmallows into Isabelle's cup without waiting for an answer. "Yes, of course I like him."

"How much?" Isabelle narrowed her eyes, waiting for Mrs. Stern's answer.

"Isabelle!" Mrs. Stern laughed. "What a question. He's a fine man, someone I've known since I was a girl. I knew his first wife too. He's been very lonely since she died. We enjoy many of the same things. He and my husband were friends. We're both over seventy, you see," Mrs. Stern said, as if that explained it all. "My heavens"—and she put her paint-spattered hands up to her pink cheeks—"but that sounds old."

"It is, kinda." Isabelle liked to call a spade a spade. "You're like Guy's grandmother. He says she's young at heart, and so are you."

"Why, Isabelle, what a nice thing to say. I'm touched. How is Guy? Such a nice little fellow, so kind."

"Oh, he's a regular hotshot now," Isabelle said. "Him and Bernie are raising worms. Money back if you don't catch anything."

Isabelle bit off a chunk of cuticle and chewed on it vigorously. "I helped Guy get out of being a goody-goody, you see," she explained. "I helped him change his image. That's what you call it, image. Nobody teases him anymore."

"Of course, dear," said Mrs. Stern absentmindedly. "That *was* nice of you to help Guy. I see I'm out of cocoa. Perhaps you'd like a nice glass of milk."

"No, thanks." Isabelle scooped the two marshmallows out of the cup. "I'll just eat 'em plain if it's all right with you."

"Oh, I have so much to do," said Mrs. Stern happily. "I don't know where to begin. Yes, of course, dear."

Isabelle saw that Mrs. Stern was too busy to talk. But before she split, Isabelle told Mrs. Stern about Sally Smith's postcard.

"Sally Smith wrote to everybody but me." Isabelle did a slow soft shoe, arms dangling loosely at her sides, to show she didn't really care. "She promised she'd write me. Maybe she lost my address. Or she forgot the zip. If she forgot the zip, that's fatal. I'll never get it. Too bad. Sally was my friend."

"Maybe I'll have a party," said Mrs. Stern, counting her knives and forks. "We could have my chicken pie. It's been so long since I've had people in."

Mrs. Stern was a little spaced out today, Isabelle could see. She said good-bye and, halfway down the path, she realized she'd forgotten to take a handful of Oreos. They'd get stale sitting on that plate. Maybe she should go back. No. If she did that, Mrs. Stern would think she was greedy.

Which she was.

But she didn't want Mrs. Stern to *think* she was.

Across the street, the Brady kids were playing fairy princess. Isabelle went over to spy on them through the hedge.

The littlest Brady, draped in some old lace curtains, was pushing Betty, the dog, in a beat-up old red wagon. Betty had aged, Isabelle thought, squinting through the hedge. Or maybe it was the pink woolen bonnet tied under Betty's hairy chin that made her look so old.

The second Brady kid, the bossy one, Isabelle knew from experience, waved her stick wand furiously and shouted orders.

"Be home by midnight!" she bellowed. "Else you'll turn into an old warty frog that's so ugly the prince will throw you out of the carriage and you'll get stomped on by a slimy, fire-breathing dragon who'll eat you up in one gulp!"

The littlest Brady let go of the wagon, raised her face to the sky, and howled like a banshee. Isabelle seized the moment and pounced from her hiding place to turn a series of really excellent cartwheels on the Bradys' lawn. She managed to do an even dozen before collapsing in a heap. The littlest Brady, recovered from her fit, calmly pushed the wagon over to where Isabelle lay and said, "This is my baby, Elvis."

"I thought your dog's name was Betty," Isabelle

said. The dog's tail thumped rhythmically against the wagon's side, and she rolled her big brown eyes at Isabelle, as if to say, "Help!"

Isabelle jumped to her feet. "You let her out of there," she said. "That's mean. Look at her. She's crying."

"Betty ran away," the bossy Brady said. "Besides, dogs don't cry."

"That's what you think." Isabelle poked a finger at the kid. "Let her out of there this minute. If you don't, I'm reporting you to the ASPCA. No wonder Betty ran away. Who wouldn't. How'd you like to be tied up with a stupid bonnet on?"

The dog's tail thumped harder, and it seemed to smile at Isabelle.

"There, there, Elvis," the bossy Brady said, and pushed the dog back down, where it lay, rolling its eyes, rapidly losing hope.

"How come you call it Elvis?" Isabelle couldn't help asking.

The bossy one shouted joyfully, "Because he ain't nuthing but a hound dog, that's why!"

"You're some smart alec, know that?" Isabelle said in her sourest voice.

The two Bradys, as if on signal, stuck out their tongues at Isabelle, who stuck hers out in return.

Then the bossy one sang "You Ain't Nuthin' But a Hound Dog" and waggled her hips, à la Elvis Presley, and Isabelle, realizing she'd been had, turned and ran the fifty-yard dash for home.

28

SIX

"Your friend Frannie was here," Isabelle's mother said. "I asked her to come in and wait for you, but she said she had to go home. She'll come back, she said. Where does she live?"

"She's not my friend," Isabelle said. "I don't even know her. I don't know where she lives, either. Except with her aunt, who's not really her aunt, she told me. She only wants her to call her her aunt."

"How old is she?" her mother wanted to know. "She looks about seven or eight, but she seems older than that, doesn't she?"

"She looks pretty young to me," said Isabelle. "A lot younger 'n me. She's small for her age, probably. And plenty fresh, too."

"Isabelle, don't be so insensitive. How would you like to be all alone in the world?" her mother said.

"Frannie's not all alone. She's got a mother," Isabelle said. "She's only a half orphan. Her mother's out looking for a new daddy on account of her old daddy died."

"I know, you told me," Isabelle's mother said.

"Yeah, well, I didn't tell you the rest. Frannie's mother got all doozied up and put a really fresh bumper sticker on her new car. That bumper sticker is so fresh, Mom, I wouldn't dare tell you what it says." And Isabelle let her eyes go all big and solemn so her mother would imagine all kinds of fresh stuff. Nothing she liked better than to fuel her mother's already vivid imagination by telling her just so much, and no more.

"What did the bumper sticker say?" Isabelle's mother asked, as Isabelle had known she would.

"I can't tell you, Mom," Isabelle said. "You'd freak."

"All right, then." Her mother was miffed; Isabelle could see. "It takes quite a lot to make me freak, miss. But put yourself in Frannie's shoes. Try to imagine how you'd feel if anything happened to me or Daddy. Or Philip."

Isabelle leaped up and hopped around the room like a kangaroo on a pogo stick. "That's what I'd do if anything happened to Philip!" she shouted.

"Watch it!" Isabelle's mother rescued a teetering lamp in the nick of time.

"That's enough, Isabelle," she said crossly. "Remember, he's your brother and someday you and he will be good friends."

"Aaarrrgh," Isabelle cried, grabbing herself by the throat and staggering in circles with her tongue hanging out, looking like a dog who's been chasing a rabbit.

"Isabelle, you are too much, you really are," her mother said, laughing in spite of herself.

"But when I get really sad is when I think about if you and Dad got knocked off by a flying saucer or something and Philip was in charge. Boy, that's when I cry buckets," Isabelle said. "On account of Philip would beat up on me even before breakfast. He'd beat up on me so much I'd be all black and blue and you could hardly see my real skin I'd be so black and blue and he'd tie me to a stake in the backyard and make me eat sour milk and turnips until I croaked."

Isabelle was so moved by the picture she'd drawn that she took a piece of paper towel and blew her nose noisily.

"Turnips," Herbie said in a hollow voice.

"Come on in, Herb," Isabelle said, opening the door. "You don't have to stand out there eavesdropping."

"I hate turnips," Herbie announced, coming in. "If I ate them every day, I'd just as soon vomit. That's why I hate Thanksgiving, on account of turnips. My mother says it's not Thanksgiving without turnips.

31

She says the Pilgrims really loved turnips. How does she know? All I can say is, the Pilgrims must've been off their rockers if they loved turnips."

"You want to fight awhile?" Isabelle asked, trying to cheer Herbie up.

"Yeah, okay, that'd be good," Herbie said. "I was feeling fine until you mentioned turnips. They depress me. Maybe we better fight in your yard today, Iz. My mother's expecting company, and she doesn't want our yard messed up."

"How about my yard?" Isabelle's mother said, but no one paid any attention.

Herbie and Isabelle had just started to mix it up when an old-fashioned, oversized pram came up the street. Pushing it was Frannie, who stopped to watch as Herbie jumped up and down on Isabelle's stomach as if she were a trampoline.

"Ugh! Oooff! Help, he's killing me!" Isabelle bellowed.

Frannie just stood there as Herbie continued his assault.

"Hey, Frannie, get this turnip offa me, will ya?" Isabelle cried.

"No siree!" Herbie said quietly. Herbie was always quiet when he was winning. "You're not pulling that phony stuff on me again, Iz. I'm wise to your tricks." Once bitten, twice shy, as Herbie's grandmother said. He went back to his trampoline bounce.

Then he heard a little tinny voice say, "But how?"

and for one fatal second his attention was diverted. He turned to look and Isabelle, using her splendid big feet, tossed Herbie skyward, and by the time he hit the turf, she was upright again.

"You can't trust boys," she told Frannie, brushing herself off. "They cheat."

Then she noticed that the pram Frannie was pushing was full of what looked like an oversized load of arms and legs. Grimy, scabby arms and legs which, on closer inspection, turned out to be two little boys.

"Who are these bozos?" Isabelle asked.

"They're my guys," Frannie said proudly. "Three's four, and Zeus, he's almost two. Say hi, guys."

"Why do you call him Three?" Isabelle wanted to know.

Frannie lifted her shoulders and said, "And baby makes three," as if that explained it. There was, apparently, no question Frannie didn't have an answer to.

"Aren't they kind of old for those things?" Isabelle asked, pointing to the pacifiers that stuck out of each boy's mouth. Three's was a sickly pink color and Zeus's a nasty shade of yellow.

"I thought only babies sucked on those things," Isabelle said.

"What's it to you, old dodo?" Three spoke around the pacifier, which bobbed up and down as he talked.

"That Three," Frannie said with a proud smile. "He can be real fresh at times. Aunt Ruth says if they suck on pacifiers, they won't suck their thumbs. Plus it keeps 'em quiet. Right, guys?"

Three made a horrible face, and his pacifier zoomed from one side of his mouth to the other.

"See that? That's a trick he learned. Smart, huh? Do it again," Frannie commanded. But Three had performed once and that was that. Zeus waggled his fingers at Isabelle and said not a word.

"If you want," Frannie said with the air of bestowing a great favor, "you can push 'em around the block. Five cents for once around." She shoved the pram at Isabelle.

"What would I want to do that for?" Isabelle asked, astonished at the idea. "That's crazy."

"Lots of people want to push my guys around," Frannie said smugly. "They like to pretend those cute little buggers are their children and they're the mothers. I have special rates for steady customers. Half an hour for a dime. Plus"—Frannie fluttered her eyelashes—"we have weekly rates too, if you're interested."

"I coulda pushed a dog named Elvis around today if I wanted," Isabelle said, sucking on a piece of her hair. "He had on this baby's bonnet, and he was cute as a bug. Cuter'n those bozos," and she smiled sweetly at Three, who stared back at her, his eyes as hard and expressionless as two black olives in his wide face.

"A dog named Elvis!" Frannie said. "What a dumb name for a dog. Why'd they call him that?"

Isabelle leaped in the air and clicked her heels in imitation of Mary Eliza Shook showing off her ballet skills.

"Because he ain't nuthing but a hound dog, that's why!" Isabelle cried, trying not to laugh out loud.

SEVEN

Halfway down, in her search for the great white shark, the idea hit. It was so perfect, so right, so excellent that Isabelle opened her mouth and hollered, "Yo!" and swallowed half the bath water.

Choking, gasping, she came up, smiling at her own cleverness.

She would take little orphan Frannie over to meet Mrs. Stern. She would put her arm protectively around Frannie's thin shoulders and lead her up the walk and through Mrs. Stern's tomato-red door.

"And who is this?" Mrs. Stern would ask, silver eyes sparkling a welcome.

"This is my friend little orphan Frannie," Isabelle planned to reply. "I'm being kind to her."

No. That wouldn't do. If she said, "I'm being kind to her," that would be rude and crude. Better to show, not tell. In her every gesture Isabelle would show Mrs. Stern how kind she was being to little waif Frannie. Mrs. Stern would be impressed by Isabelle's kindness. She would then know that Isabelle was a far kinder person than other people. Especially Guy Gibbs.

"Yeah! Yeah!" Isabelle shouted, and in her excitement she sent a series of giant waves over the tub's side and onto the bathroom floor.

"Oh, boy!" Isabelle took a look.

"It wasn't my fault," she said aloud, as if her mother had been standing there, saying, "Not again! How many times have I warned you, Isabelle? Look what you've done."

"I'll clean it all up," she said, and hopped out of the tub. She'd mop up every drop with the already sodden bath mat as well as the unused towels. She'd clean it up before her mother and father got home. They'd gone to the movies with their friends the Bascombs. When her father learned the movie was rated PG, he said, "Does that stand for 'pretty good'?" as her mother dragged him to the car.

Isabelle put on her pajamas and robe and went into

her room and wrote on her blackboard: "ISABELLE IS A GENUS."

She stood back to study her work. The spelling wasn't perfect, but the thought was there. Then she tiptoed downstairs. Since Philip had taken up talking to girls on the telephone when he was in charge, Isabelle had much more freedom of movement. She could roam through the house, and as long as Philip was busy on the phone, she could do anything she felt like.

"Far out!" she heard Philip yodel. "That blows my mind." Then she heard him laugh and pound the couch cushions. Philip liked to stretch out on the couch and make himself comfortable while telephoning.

Inside the refrigerator was a half-eaten bowl of Jello and a leg of lamb. The freezer was empty of ice cream. Lucky she wasn't really hungry, Isabelle decided. Back upstairs, she took a pair of her mother's panty hose from the drawer, slipped it over her face, and picked up the phone, very quietly so Philip wouldn't hear. He had hung up. Good.

Isabelle dialed a number. "Shook residence, Mary Eliza Shook speaking," a voice said.

"May I please speak to Mary Eliza Shook?" Isabelle said from behind the panty hose mask.

"If it's you again, Isabelle," said Mary Eliza crossly, "you're going to get it. My father said next time you called us up he was going to report you to the police. He said you're a public nuisance."

Isabelle took several deep breaths, filling her lungs

with air. Then she swallowed noisily, which always made her voice darker, and said, from behind her mother's panty hose mask, "You have won the lottery. You, Mary Eliza Shook, have won the lottery."

There was a short silence, then the air was filled with the sound of Mary Eliza's joyful scream. Isabelle covered her ear with her hand and let Mary Eliza scream.

"I won, I won, I won!" screamed Mary Eliza.

"Bring your winning ticket down to the office Monday morning," Isabelle said in a gruff voice. "You have to have the winning ticket, else it's all off."

"How much do I get?" Mary Eliza gasped.

"Let me put it through the computer. Hang on," and Isabelle put down the receiver and paced around the room for several minutes. She fancied she could hear Mary Eliza breathing through the phone. Then she went back and said, "After taxes, it comes to one hundred billion million. Dollars, that is."

"Who is this?" It was Mary Eliza's father speaking. Softly, ever so gently, Isabelle hung up. When she went back to get the pail and mop, Philip was on the telephone again.

"Just go with the flow," Philip advised. "Just go for it. With the flow." Isabelle trudged up and swabbed down the bathroom floor, pretending she was a sailor aboard ship, cleaning the decks. It was hard work. The more she swabbed, the more water there was. Or so it seemed. Finally, she stuffed all the wet towels and the bath mat into the pail and carried it back down to the washing machine.

"Get caught in a typhoon?" Philip asked her. "You look waterlogged, babe.

"I know." He snapped his fingers. "You went skin diving again and flooded the floor, right? Right. Oh, boy, are you gonna get it. Are they ever gonna lash you to the mast," Philip chortled.

The telephone rang and Philip got to it first, as usual.

"Yeah," he said. Then his voice changed abruptly, deepened and aged. Philip was a good mimic. Isabelle stood and listened to him turn into his father.

"Yes, it's him. Sure. Oh, is that so?" He stared at Isabelle as he listened. "I'm sorry to hear that . . . . Yes, indeed, I'll take care of it. I'll see to it she doesn't bother you again. Thanks for calling." He hung up and a slow smile came over his face.

"Guess who that was, rug rat," Philip said. "Just take one guess."

Isabelle tossed the soaking towels and mat into the washing machine. "Who?" she said.

"Mr. Shook, baby. Father of Mary Eliza. Wanted to talk to Dad. I pretended I was Dad and he bought it. I said I'd speak to you. He said you'd been making a nuisance of yourself calling up there all the time. He said he wants it to stop."

Philip put an experimental finger up his nose, withdrew it and frowned, as if trying to decide what it was he'd extracted. Then he threw it at Isabelle. He was always doing that, pulling big goobers from his nose and throwing them at her. Mostly they were nothing, only pretend goobers. But she could never be quite sure.

To be safe, she ducked.

"Are you going to tell?" Isabelle asked.

Philip shrugged, nonchalant, enjoying himself. "Who knows? I think I'll just hold it over your head for a while, like an ax. Blackmail, toots. Good, old-fashioned blackmail. One false step and it's kneecap time, weirdo."

Isabelle went upstairs and got the nail scissors out of her mother's drawer to cut her bangs. They turned out sort of ragged and spiky looking, better than she'd planned. Maybe she'd dye her hair pink and glue red feathers in it, like a punk rocker. And get herself a sleeveless T-shirt that lit up when you pressed a button, spelling out: "BLOOD."

Cool.

Snip, snip, the hair over her ears fell without a whisper. Now she was ready for three earrings in her left ear—two stars and one gold safety pin.

The effect was dazzling.

Isabelle heard the garage door close. Her mother and father were home. She made it into bed just in time. In the dark she ran her hands over her head. It felt funny, sort of prickly and bald in spots. And in spite of the remnants of her hair that scurried around inside her pajamas like a gang of mice at a disco, Isabelle fell into a deep, untroubled sleep.

EIGHT

"I can't stay but a minute," Aunt Maude said, *teetering* up the walk in her little high-heeled shoes. "My, but that sermon was boring. What on earth!" Aunt Maude pressed her little hand over her heart. "Your hair, child. What have you done to your hair?"

Without waiting for Isabelle to answer, she settled herself in, wriggling her rear end until she was comfortable, and said, "I know. It's one of those punk rock hairdos. Next thing is to dye your hair pink and put an arrow through your head or your nose or some such. I saw one of those punk people on TV, and he was wearing a frog mask and boxer shorts made of aluminum foil. Most extraordinary, I must say. The things that go on these days. Be good to your mother and father, Isabelle, because they have a lot to deal with."

Isabelle opened her mouth to reply, but Aunt Maude plunged on.

"Don't think I don't keep up with things because I do," she said. "What is that gorgeous smell?"

They went through this every Sunday. Aunt Maude always said she couldn't possibly stay to dinner. She always stayed.

"Maude darling, how lovely to see you." Isabelle admired the way her father seemed astonished at Aunt Maude's presence. He hugged her against his white apron and said, "You must stay for dinner, Maude. I'm doing roast chicken with forty cloves of garlic."

"Oh, I couldn't! Forty cloves of garlic! Naughty boy." Aunt Maude shook a playful finger. "We'll all smell to high heaven."

"Does that mean you're staying?" Isabelle asked.

"That puts me in mind of my dear father," Aunt Maude said, ignoring Isabelle's question. "As he got on in years, his memory failed. The doctor put him on garlic pills as garlic is supposed to be good for the memory. My father took the pills for some time until one day he said to my mother, 'What am I taking these pills for, Mary?' "

44

Both Aunt Maude and Isabelle's father seemed to find this story very funny. Isabelle laughed too, although she didn't think it was *that* funny.

"Nobody's said a word about my new hat," Aunt Maude said.

"It's a standout, all right," Isabelle's father said gallantly. "What exactly do you call it?"

"Looks like a hard hat to me," said Isabelle.

Aunt Maude crowed, "The child's right! It *is* a hard hat. How clever of you, dear. The young woman down the block had a garage sale. That's a tag sale, only you have it in your garage, you see. I got there early, to catch the worm, so to speak, and there was this adorable yellow hat sitting on the card table. I knew in an instant I had to have it. The woman's husband is a repair man for the telephone company. This was his old hat, which he wore to protect himself from falling objects, falling out of trees and so on. As you can see"—Aunt Maude turned slowly, showing them—"it has 'Telephone Company' written on it. So I solved that by putting tape over the letters and then this little veil around it to add the final touch. I tried it on and everyone agreed it was *me*, don't you know. Plus, she took fifty percent off the price, and that decided me. Don't you think it's chic?"

"Some chick," Isabelle made a little joke, but she was cut off by a loud, ominous noise. She looked up in time to see a large piece of the living room ceiling descending slowly, ever so slowly, it seemed to her, almost like a balloon.

Crash! Plunk! Boom! The ceiling landed dead center on Aunt Maude's new hard hat.

Aunt Maude opened and closed her mouth several times, like a fish, then closed her eyes. Isabelle's mother came running to help her father drag Aunt Maude to safety. Plaster dust filled the air, filled Isabelle's eyes and nose and throat until she could hardly breathe.

"It's a bomb!" Philip shouted. "Somebody planted a bomb! Call the cops! The terrorists have landed!"

"Cool it, Philip," Isabelle's mother said. "Are you all right, Maude? Get a glass of water, Philip, hurry."

Presently Aunt Maude opened her eyes. Outside of looking a little woozier than usual, she seemed unharmed.

"Anything broken?" Isabelle's father brushed her off and set her upright.

"It was fate," said Aunt Maude, shaking her head, the hat still on it. "What a blessing this dear little hat is. It saved my life."

Everyone looked at the hard hat, which was scarcely dented, and agreed.

"I can't imagine what happened," Aunt Maude sighed, smiling around at them.

"I think I can," said Isabelle's father in a menacing tone. He turned to glare at Isabelle, who was seriously thinking of hitch-hiking to Australia.

46

"The bathtub overflowed last night, is that right?" he asked her. "When you were skin diving again. Which you've been warned about repeatedly. Is that it?"

All eyes were on Isabelle. Usually she found this pleasant, but not this time. It was her fault. They knew that; she knew that.

"I guess so," Isabelle whispered. "Unless maybe it *was* a bomb." Nobody spoke.

"There I was, sitting quietly, smelling the delicious chicken with sixty cloves of garlic," Aunt Maude said, as if they hadn't all been on the scene, "when suddenly this terrible crashing sound came and . . ."

Isabelle decided this was the time to split. The time to put space between herself and home. Give them time to cool off.

She slipped out quietly. The air was fresh and full of promise of all kinds of exciting things.

"Hey," she heard Philip whisper, "the weird chick's back, hanging around the back door. I told her you were dead meat, but last time I looked, she was still there."

Dead meat is right, Isabelle thought, heading for the back door. Maybe she could lie low at Frannie's house until the whole thing blew over.

NINE

"I'm outa here!" Isabelle cried, pouncing on Frannie, who was sitting on the stoop tossing pebbles in the air.

"What smells so good?" Frannie asked.

"Eighty cloves of garlic," Isabelle replied. "Let's go see Mrs. Stern."

"Normally, I don't like garlic," Frannie said, "but it smells good."

"Mrs. Stern always gives me cocoa and marshmallows," Isabelle said.

Reluctantly Frannie agreed to go to Mrs. Stern's.

"After, let's go to your house," Isabelle suggested. She was dying to see Frannie's house.

"Can't," Frannie said flatly. "Sunday's a day of rest. Aunt Ruth likes to put her feet up and play cards. She likes her peace and quiet on Sundays."

"What about your creepy little brothers? I notice you're not pushing 'em around today. Do you lock 'em up on Sundays?"

"What brothers?" Frannie said.

"The two little creeps, Zeus and Three. In the carriage." Isabelle wondered if she'd made them up. "You said I could push 'em around the block for a nickel."

"Oh, them. They're not brothers, they're just kids. Their mother drops them off when she goes to work. They board at our house sometimes."

"I thought they were your brothers. How come I never see you at school? What grade are you in? Who's your teacher? Mine's Mrs. Esposito. She's the best teacher in the whole school."

"I don't go to school," Frannie said airily. "My mother said I didn't have to bother with school as long as we're not sticking around here long. Maybe I'll go when we get to Michigan."

"Michigan? Way out there? How come?"

"My mother called last night. She said she met this guy who has a Toyota agency in Michigan, and she thinks he might be the one. Her horoscope said she was due for a change in her life-style, and she figures Michigan might be it."

Isabelle chewed on the inside of her cheek, secretly envying Frannie her laid-back life-style, so different from her own.

"How old are you anyway?" she asked Frannie.

"How old are you?" Frannie replied.

"I'm ten. How about you?"

Frannie stopped walking and stared up at the sky. Isabelle looked up to see what she was staring at. A clump of clouds scudded across the sky, like little lost sheep trying to catch up with their shepherd.

"I'm approximately eight," Frannie said at last. "I'm not exactly sure. My mother was only a child when I was born."

"How big of a child?" Isabelle asked.

"Oh, about fifteen or sixteen. She could've put me up for adoption, you see." Frannie looked directly at Isabelle for the first time. "She had tons of offers from people who wanted me because I was so adorable. She could've got big bucks for me, about a thousand dollars, but she kept me instead. Only she doesn't remember exactly when I was born. My father was away when I was born. He was serving his country, and the hospital lost the records, so we don't know for sure when my birthday is."

"Then how do you know when to have your birthday party?" Isabelle demanded, standing stock-still in amazement. She'd never known anyone who didn't know when their own birthday was.

"Oh, we don't bother with birthday parties," Frannie said with a little smile on her face. Her eyes were as round as an owl's and as wise. "Birthdays cost money, after all. And, what's more, my mother's allergic to ice cream. Plus, it makes you fat. Once we had a cake, though."

On they went. Isabelle walked slowly, sorting out all this information.

"I never heard of anyone who was allergic to ice cream," she said at last.

"If you ask me," Frannie said, "there's lots of things you never heard of. How come your brother said you were dead meat? That's not very nice."

"He's a big goofball," said Isabelle. "Don't listen to anything he says."

A strange car was parked in Mrs. Stern's driveway. When Isabelle knocked, a man came to the door.

"Is Mrs. Stern home?" Isabelle asked.

"She is but she's dressing," he said. "May I ask who's calling?" The man had gray hair, a red necktie, and a nice face.

"I'm Isabelle. Are you her brother?"

"No, I'm just a friend," he said, smiling. "I'll see if she's presentable." They stood on the steps twiddling their thumbs.

"What do you want to bet he's her boyfriend,"

Frannie said in a piercing whisper.

"She's too old for a boyfriend," Isabelle said sharply.

"That's what you think."

"Oh, Isabelle, come in, do," Mrs. Stern said. She had on an extremely blue dress and shoes with heels. "You look nice," Isabelle said, although she preferred Mrs. Stern in paint-spattered jeans and sneakers with holes in the toes.

"Thank you," Mrs. Stern said. "John, this is my friend Isabelle, my sometime paper boy and friend. I wouldn't know what to do without Isabelle," and she laid her hand on Isabelle's shoulder.

Isabelle remembered her manners. "This is Frannie," she said. "She's an orphan. Her old daddy died and . . ." Isabelle slipped a kind arm around Frannie.

"Let me tell," Frannie whispered, pinching Isabelle on the arm, hard, so that Isabelle gave a little yelp and let go. "It's my story. I should tell it, not you." Frannie turned to Mrs. Stern and recited, "I'm a norphan, you see," and Mrs. Stern said, "Poor darling," giving Frannie her complete attention in the way she had.

John looked at his watch.

"Ada, I'm afraid it's getting late, we'll have to go," he said. "Our reservation's for noon."

"Of course. I do want to hear about you, Frannie. Come back soon, girls, will you? We'll have a party. Maybe some cupcakes and . . ."

"Come along, Ada," and John ushered Mrs. Stern out to the car, placed her inside as if she were a valuable package, and firmly slammed the door. Then he got in, and they peeled off.

Isabelle and Frannie stood and watched them go.

"I told you he was her boyfriend," Frannie said.

"Big deal," answered Isabelle, disappointed at this turn of events.

"That's not a new Caddy," Frannie said knowledgeably. "Probably it's about five, six years old."

"Who cares?" said Isabelle.

Across the street the bossy Brady hollered.

"Catch him, catch him!" she shouted as Elvis, bonnet dangling, streaked by, ears laid back, tail flying, on the way to freedom.

"I'm outa here," Isabelle said sourly, stalking off.

"Dead meat, dead meat!" Frannie called after her, but she didn't look back, not once.

TEN

"*So now I'm grounded for two weeks. They only let me* out to go to school. Plus, no flippers, no mask, no skin diving. No baths. No nothing."

"Well, at least you get out of taking a bath," said Herbie, looking on the bright side.

"Showers," Isabelle said, shrugging. "And I might have to help pay for a new ceiling. That's what my father said. But it was so funny, Herb. If you'd been there, you woulda cracked up. Aunt Maude looked so funny with part of the ceiling on her head. I almost

54

laughed. Lucky thing I didn't. My father might've tarred and feathered me and run me outa town on a rail. Lucky for her she had on her hard hat. Aunt Maude is into funny hats."

"You're telling me," Herbie said.

"My mother's taking me for a haircut today," Isabelle said. "To make me look human, she said. She's putting André to work on me."

"Get him to shave your head, why don't you?" Herbie suggested. "I'd shave mine, but my mother said if I did, she'd send me to camp for the whole summer. Until it growed out. I hate camp. All you do is make lanyards."

" 'Grewed out,' not 'growed out,' " Isabelle corrected.

"So now you're Mrs. Esposito," Herbie said. "Think of all the time you'd save if your head was shaved. When you got up you wouldn't have to comb your hair or anything."

On the way to the hairdresser, Isabelle thought briefly of doing her imitation of a police car siren. One look at her mother's face, however, and she decided not to. Her mother and father had been pretty uptight since the ceiling fell on Aunt Maude.

"André, this is my daughter Isabelle," her mother said. "See what you can do, will you?"

André circled Isabelle, regarding her with narrowed eyes. "It is indeed a challenge," he said. "André loves a challenge. Sit," he ordered Isabelle, as if she were a dog who'd just graduated from obedience school. "Sit. And be absolutely still."

She sat, and André threw a large white towel over her so only her head showed.

"Now. One move and I will not be responsible for what occurs," André said. "One move and I might take off one of your ears, and that would not be nice." He smiled at Isabelle in a tight-lipped way, and she knew he meant business.

"If you picked up my ear and rushed me to the hospital they could sew it back on and it would work good as new," Isabelle said. "I've heard about that happening to people. And how about that famous painter who cut off his ear? He kept on painting, like nothing had happened."

André bared his teeth like the wolf in Little Red Riding Hood. "One does not paint with one's ear, isn't it so?"

"Could you make me look like a punker, please?" Isabelle asked.

But André did not answer, so absorbed was he in cutting Isabelle's hair. His scissors flashed, skimmed the back of her neck, and she fell silent, watching torrents of hair fall from her head. She put out a hand to catch some, and André shrieked, "I said still! I will not tolerate the movement. I will make of you the little gamin."

Isabelle shut her eyes and thought about how she could pay for the ceiling. She could try a lemonade

56

stand, but it wasn't hot enough yet. She could baby-sit only she didn't know of anyone who'd hire her.

"Denise," André called sharply, "see if Mrs. Boop is dry. And, Denise, please, no more gum. This is not a shop for chewing gum."

"You sound just like my teacher," Isabelle said.

Isabelle longed to scratch the back of her itchy neck, but she didn't dare. No telling what André might do.

"So now." He whipped off the towel and handed her a mirror. "See if André has not made another miracle. From ugly duckling to swan, in"—he consulted his heavy gold wristwatch—"a mere fourteen minutes. A record, even for such a one as André."

"I look like a boy," Isabelle said, not displeased.

"From waif to gamin. Ah, an adorable boy, it is true," and André snapped his fingers.

"Denise, the broom. I must check the color on the countess. Sweep."

Isabelle took the broom from Denise's unresisting hand. "I love to sweep," she said. "Boy, that's a lot of hair. I could use it for something, only I don't know what." She wielded the broom with a flourish.

"Want a job, kid?" Denise asked, yawning. "You got it. Minimum wage and half an hour for lunch."

Before Isabelle could reply, André came steaming back. "Denise, see to Mrs. Boop. She is very upset. She has been abandoned under the dryer. Soothe her. Take out her rollers. Give her a cup of tea. Anything. I will be there in the instant."

57

"You mean it, Denise?" Isabelle stopped sweeping to ask. "You're serious?"

"Why not?" said Denise, filing her nails in a languorous fashion, Mrs. Boop or no.

"How much is minimum wage anyway?" asked Isabelle.

ELEVEN

The man came to fix the ceiling.

"What's the damage come to?" Isabelle asked him.

"Plenty," the man said. "You responsible for this here?" and he jerked his thumb upward.

Isabelle pretended she hadn't heard and charged noisily up the stairs. "USE YOUR IMAGINATION," she wrote on her blackboard. That's what Mrs. Esposito was always telling the class.

"Your imagination's like a muscle," Mrs. Esposito had said. "The more it's used, the better it works. Use it every day. Keep it well oiled, like your bicycle or your lawn mower." Isabelle rather liked that. She imagined herself pushing her imagination around the yard or down the street. Or up the steepest hill.

Mary Eliza's hand shot up.

"Yes, Mary Eliza. What is it?"

Mary Eliza hoisted her rear end up from her seat and said, as if it were a whole new idea and totally hers, "Your imagination's like a muscle in your head."

"Yeah, and just as hard," said Chauncey from behind his grimy hand. Chauncey was definitely feeling his oats these days, Isabelle thought as the class tittered. She stacked her fists on her desk and rested her chin on them and, without moving her head, slipped her eyes from side to side, to see what was what. Not a whole lot. Herbie was chewing gum, working on his phony boil, no doubt. Mary Eliza was busily scribbling in a little black book.

"Let your imagination soar, children," Mrs. Esposito said. "Like a kite. Let it go as high as it will. The sky's the limit."

It was a grand thought.

Now "ONCE UPON A TIME," Isabelle wrote on the blackboard. That was her favorite beginning. Anything could happen. Unfortunately, no other words came. She must be suffering from writer's block.

"Once upon a time," Isabelle said out loud.

Outside her door someone coughed. Isabelle hid in her closet in case it was a burglar. Or a fire-breathing dragon. Or her father, wanting to have A Talk. About Responsibility.

"The door was open so I just came in," said Frannie.

Isabelle sprang out of the closet and said, "I'm writing a story. Let's take turns. First I write a sentence, then you. Let your imagination soar."

"No," said Frannie, surprisingly. "I won't."

"Come on, do it," Isabelle commanded.

"Try and make me." Frannie clenched her fists and stuck out her chin. "Listen, it's your house and your blackboard. You write anything you want. But I don't have to. I'm not doing it. Even if you torture me, I won't."

Torture. It was something Isabelle hadn't even considered and now did. Once again she let her imagination soar. Drive sticks under Frannie's fingernails. Tie her to a tree on top of an anthill and pour honey on her stomach so the ants could lick it off. Hang Frannie by her thumbs.

The possibilities were endless.

"Know something? You're a brat," Frannie said. "You think everything you do is so great. You're so tough, so cool. You can't keep pushing people around. You're not a queen or a president or anything. All you are is a brat."

Then, as if somebody had pushed a button, tears fell from Frannie's eyes. Great round tears just dropped from her eyes like pebbles. They didn't slide down her cheeks, they just fell, soundlessly. Most people squinched up their face when they cried. They got red and looked ugly. Not Frannie. Her eyes stayed open and her face remained pale. Most people, when they cried, had to blow their nose. Not Frannie. She didn't so much as snuffle.

But the sounds Frannie made were the most amazing part of all. She raised her knobby wrist to her mouth and as if she were playing a musical instrument, she produced the most incredible sound Isabelle had ever heard.

Frannie wailed. The wails went up and down the scale and raised goose bumps on Isabelle's arms.

"Stop," she said. Frannie went on wailing. The sounds dismayed Isabelle, and she wondered how Frannie made them.

At last Frannie drew a long, shuddering breath and said, "I can't. Don't you see, I just can't."

"Hey," Isabelle said softly. "I'm sorry. I only wanted for us to have fun. That's all, have a good time." She patted Frannie awkwardly.

"Let's read this horse book. I just got it out of the library. It's a wonderful book, the librarian said. I'll read you a chapter, then you read me one. How's that?"

Frannie shouted "No!" and scrambled to the center of the room, where she stood, fists at the ready, knees slightly bent, ready for a fight.

"You're stupid!" she shouted. "Don't you understand?"

Isabelle shook her head, unable to speak.

"I can't write and I can't read. And if you tell any-body, I'll say I can, I'll say you're a liar, so there."

Isabelle and Frannie stared at each other. Neither said a word.

"So that's it," Isabelle said. A wonderful idea occurred to her.

"I will teach you, child," Isabelle said in her most kindly way.

"No, you won't," Frannie snapped. "I don't want you to. I won't let you teach me. I'm fine the way I am," and she marched out with her head in the air.

Isabelle listened to Frannie hurtle down the stairs, heard the front door slam.

Isabelle lay on her bed with her feet propped up on the wall and thought about Frannie not being able to read or write. How would that be, how would it feel? She could only imagine.

Then she got up and went over to her blackboard and after: "ONCE UPON A TIME," she wrote: "THERE WAS A CHILD WHO COULDN'T READ OR RIGHT."

Something was not quite right there.

Ah.

Isabelle erased "RIGHT" and wrote "WRITE" instead.

Her writer's block was over, almost before it had begun, she thought, well pleased.

TWELVE

"Who scalped you, dear?" Mary Eliza Shook *whistled,* nailing Isabelle to the girls' room wall. "You look like the moths got to you. I'm never cutting my hair. Not ever, it's my crowning glory." Mary Eliza tossed her head and sent her hair flying into Isabelle's open mouth. Isabelle clamped it shut and chomped on Mary Eliza's hair as if it were a dish of chicken nuggets with honey sauce.

"Stop!" Mary Eliza shouted and backed off.

"Yuck." Isabelle spit out some remaining strands

of Mary Eliza's hair. "Disgusting. This is a punk hair-cut, if you want to know. I'm dyeing it pink and get-ting my ears pierced, too."

"Who cares?" Mary Eliza lifted both arms and, brief-case dangling from one hand, executed several pliés and entrechats. Mary Eliza had been taking ballet lessons since she was three. It didn't seem to Isabelle she was making any progress at all.

"I've got a new tutu," Mary Eliza said. "It's pale blue and sparkly. It matches my eyes," and she shoved her face close so Isabelle could check out her eyes.

"Pale blue wards off evil spirits," Isabelle told her. "Bet you didn't know that."

"I don't know any evil spirits," Mary Eliza said, "except you." She burst out laughing, and Isabelle aimed the tip of her friendship ring at Mary Eliza's stomach and fired off a couple of random punches.

"Cut it out," said Mary Eliza crossly. "I'm allowed to ask a friend over every day this week to see my new tutu. Which day shall I put you down for?" and she rooted around inside her briefcase like a pig looking for truffles and brought forth a small black book, the one she'd been scribbling in in class.

"What's that?" Isabelle asked against her better judgment. She knew better than to show interest in Mary Eliza's possessions, but this time she was curious.

Mary Eliza's eyebrows soared. "It's my date book," she said. "It's for writing down all my dates in. Shall

I put you down for Wednesday at four P.M.?"

"Down for what?" Isabelle asked.

"For coming over to see my new tutu, of course," said Mary Eliza, pencil poised.

"Are you gonna be inside it? Because if you are, I don't want to be there. Only if it's empty." And Isabelle rocked and rolled around Mary Eliza, bobbing her head, sticking out her chin and making faces, shuffling in time to music only she could hear.

Jane Malone came into the girls' room.

"Hi, Jane," said Isabelle. "What's new?"

"I got a letter from Sally Smith yesterday," Jane said.

"A letter." Isabelle's heart fell. "A real letter?" She hadn't even gotten a postcard, and Sally Smith had promised she'd send one.

"Sure. Sally's doing fine. She cried for about a week when she got there, but now she says she'd probably cry if they said she was moving back here. She wanted to know what was happening, what was new. How about if we all write a letter to Sally? I'll begin and then you can write on the same piece of paper." Jane's face shone with pleasure at the idea.

"Neat!" said Mary Eliza, whipping out her ballpoint pen.

But Isabelle's feelings were bruised.

"I can't," she told them. "I have to go home and work on my story."

"What story? Did Mrs. Esposito give us a story assignment?" and Mary Eliza flipped open her date book one more time. "What day is it due? What's it supposed to be about? I'll write it down so I won't forget."

"This isn't anything for class," Isabelle said. "It's a story I'm writing and sending in to a magazine who might publish it. They'll pay me money and I'll get my name in print."

Mary Eliza bit her lip. Isabelle knew from the expression on her face that she wished *she'd* thought of writing a story and sending it to a magazine who would publish it and pay her for the story and put her name in the magazine.

"That's great, Isabelle," said Jane Malone. "What's the name of the magazine? Maybe I'll write a story and send it to them too."

"I forget," Isabelle said. "I've gotta split now, Jane. See you."

"I don't believe you," Mary Eliza said in a booming voice. "That's the first I heard that you can write stories for money and send them to a magazine. If anyone gets their name in a magazine, it should be me."

Isabelle flapped her elbows like a bird about to take flight and rocked and rolled around Mary Eliza some more. Who cared about old Sally Smith anyway? Sally Smith was a traitor, a breaker of promises. Who cared?

"*Rolling Stones*," Isabelle said, head bobbing, feet moving with the speed of light. "*Rolling Stones*," she said, opening the girls' room door and rocking and rolling out into the hall.

67

"Is that where she's sending it?" Mary Eliza hissed. "Is that the magazine?"

"I don't think so," Jane said doubtfully. "I think that's who she's dancing to. That's the music she's dancing to, I think."

THIRTEEN

After school Isabelle went over to Mrs. Stern's, in search of some TLC. She wanted to talk about the ceiling falling on Aunt Maude. About her plans to teach an unnamed person to read and write. And she wanted to discuss people who promised to write to her and didn't. All that and more.

Mrs. Stern was in the backyard, weeding.

"You're here in the nick of time, Isabelle," and Mrs. Stern put out a hand. "If I stayed on my knees much longer, I might never be able to get up." As Isabelle pulled her to her feet, Mrs. Stern winced. "You're never old until your knees give out. Remember that, my child."

They went inside. "I know I have a fresh box of cocoa somewhere, but to tell the truth, Isabelle, I've been on such a tear I don't know what I've got and what I don't. Oh, here it is." Mrs. Stern took out the cocoa. She poured some milk in a saucepan and stood at the stove, stirring it.

"I was so sorry to rush off the other day," Mrs. Stern said, "but John had made a reservation at the Yellow Cat and they won't hold a table if you're late. Please bring Frannie over soon. I promised you both a party. I scarcely had a chance to say hello. I hate being rushed. I seem to rush a good deal lately, what with one thing and another. Get the cups, please."

Isabelle got down the cups with a flourish. Then she opened a fresh pack of marshmallows and put one in each cup.

"It's dining and dancing and Lord knows what gallivanting with John here," Mrs. Stern said as they sat down. "I'm all worn out," and she smiled, and Isabelle could see she didn't look in the least worn out.

"John must be a party animal," Isabelle said.

"Isabelle!" Mrs. Stern exploded in laughter. "I must remember to tell him that. 'Party animal!' Wonderful."

"Has he gone for good?"

"No, he's visiting friends. He'll be back again. To

tell the truth, Isabelle, it's nice having the house to myself." Mrs. Stern drank her cocoa and left her marshmallow. Isabelle liked to hold hers in her mouth, swishing it about until she swallowed it whole.

"I like being alone," Mrs. Stern confided. "And it's a good thing, too. If you don't enjoy your own company, you're in trouble."

"Where does John live?" Isabelle asked.

"In Florida. I hate Florida. Too many old people there." They both laughed.

"John loves to go, you see. He likes to dance and go to the track to watch the horses race, and would you believe"—Mrs. Stern rolled her eyes—"he's learning to tango."

"Is that a game or what? I never heard of tango," said Isabelle.

"It's a dance, a very tricky, exotic dance. John says he'll conquer the tango before it conquers him, and he probably will."

"He must be a very nice man," Isabelle said primly. "If you like him."

"He's a lovely man." Mrs. Stern stared down into her empty cup. Isabelle could see the marshmallow sitting there, all soft and squishy, just the way she liked them.

"Isabelle, I'd like to discuss something with you, something private and something I'd like you to keep to yourself. May I?"

"Sure." Isabelle dragged her eyes away from

Mrs. Stern's marshmallow. "Shoot."

"Well, it's an adult sort of thing, and I know you're a child and I'm an old woman, but still, you seem a sensible child."

Isabelle was stunned. She'd been called many things but "sensible" was a first.

"I certainly can't tell Stella, although I must admit I'd *love* to." Stella was Mrs. Stern's sister-in-law, who was always bragging about what great shape she was in, even if she was seventeen months older than Mrs. Stern.

"If you want to borrow some money," Isabelle said, "I have forty-four dollars in my savings account."

"Bless you." Mrs. Stern's silver eyes glistened. "No, it's not money. I have enough money."

"Boy, you're probably the only person I know who does," Isabelle said.

Mrs. Stern cleared her throat and laced her fingers together. "John has asked for my hand," she said.

"Your hand? How about the rest of you?" Isabelle asked indignantly. "Didn't he ask for the rest of you?"

"That's an old-fashioned expression, Isabelle. To ask for one's hand means you want to marry the person you ask, hand and all."

Isabelle was shocked and tried not to show it. Mrs. Stern married! A bride? Bizarre.

"Well, if you gave him your hand," she said in her

new sensible fashion, "then he could live here and help you clean your gutters and weed the garden and paint and all. Then you could take it easy."

"No," said Mrs. Stern. "We would go to live in his condo in Florida, and John said I'd never have to do another lick of work in my life. Everything would be done for us. For me."

"Would you like that?"

"Well, no. No, I don't think so. As a matter of fact"—Mrs. Stern tapped the table with her finger—"I think I'd hate it. It's odd how sometimes if you put things into words, you get a clearer picture, isn't it?"

Isabelle knew Mrs. Stern didn't expect an answer, so she clammed up and only nodded in her sensible way.

"Yes, I think I'd absolutely hate it," Mrs. Stern said. "I thank you, Isabelle, for your help. You've been a great help." Mrs. Stern smiled. "Now I must get back to the weeds before they take over."

"Sure." Isabelle got up. "Mrs. Stern, if you're not going to eat your marshmallow, can I have it?" she asked.

"It's the least I can do," said Mrs. Stern. "Take it and how about one more for the road?"

Isabelle skipped home. She hadn't skipped in a while and had forgotten how good skipping made her feel. She hadn't told Mrs. Stern any of the things she'd planned to tell her. She'd only listened to Mrs. Stern's problems. She'd been a great help. She was a sensible child. She was making progress, no matter what anyone said.

FOURTEEN

Frannie was perched on the back step, waiting, when Isabelle chugged up the drive.

"I can stay tonight," Frannie announced. "For supper. Like your mother said. I asked my aunt and she said it'd suit her a treat on account of she's hosting a Tupperware party, and she said she needs to clean up the joint."

"I don't know. I better ask," said Isabelle. She decided on her way inside to take the positive approach and tell instead.

"Frannie can stay for supper tonight," she told her mother.

It was not a good time. Isabelle could see that. Her mother's hair and face were both frazzled. She'd been working on her word processor all day, and she was losing the battle. It was new and she said she was going to master it if it killed her.

"Oh, not tonight, kids. Sorry, Frannie. We'll be lucky if we *eat* supper at all tonight. The way it looks now it's bread and milk for everyone." Then she took a look at Frannie and said, "How about coming for Sunday dinner? We always have a gala feast then. Isabelle's father fixes dinner on Sunday. We'd love to have you, Frannie. Think you can come?"

"Well," Frannie said, "I guess. But I can stay tonight too."

"Sunday's better," Isabelle's mother stated, and went back to her work.

"What time?" Frannie asked.

"About twelve thirty, after church," Isabelle said.

"What's he fixing?" Frannie said.

Isabelle's mother rested her chin in her hands and rolled her eyes. "It's a secret. That's what makes it so exciting. It's always something special."

"Yeah, and Aunt Maude usually stays too," Isabelle told Frannie. "As a matter of fact, she always stays although she pretends she won't. Aunt Maude's a real aunt, though. Not a phony one, like yours."

"Who says Aunt Ruth's a phony?" Frannie demanded angrily.

"You said," Isabelle replied. "You said she wants you to call her aunt, but she's not a real aunt. So I call that a phony."

"You've got no business calling her a phony," Frannie said, fists clenched. "You don't even know her. If I come on Sunday"—Frannie had calmed down some—"I'll wear my new frock. It's a real frock, all right. I look like a movie star in that frock. I look like somebody in a game show. That's what Aunt Ruth says."

"What's a frock?" Isabelle asked.

Frannie's mouth dropped open and her eyes popped in astonishment.

"You don't know what a frock is?" Frannie said. "It's this really special dress; you only bring it out for dressy parties. My mother sent it to me from Detroit. Did I tell you my mother's boyfriend gave her a diamond?"

Isabelle and her mother shook their heads no, she hadn't told them.

"Well"—Frannie licked her lips—"it's about a karat, set in platinum with lots of little diamonds on the sides and all around. Now my mother says she can't do the dishes or anything, on account of the diamond. Her hands were made for diamonds, and a diamond's a big responsibility, you see."

"Right you are," Isabelle's mother agreed. "Now,

girls, mind taking off? I'm very busy with this thing."

"Come on, let's go," Isabelle said, and they tiptoed outside.

"How come she calls it supper when it's a school day or something," Frannie asked, "and when it's Sunday she calls it dinner? What's the dif?"

Isabelle spread her hands, fingers fanned wide.

"It's very simple," she said. "Supper is when she cooks it, dinner's when he does."

FIFTEEN

"Such a strange little girl I met outside just now," Aunt Maude said, taking off her gloves. "When I admired her dress, she said, 'This is not a dress, it's a frock,' and when I told her I once had one very like hers, she ran away. Though mine, of course, had a little ruffle right here," and Aunt Maude showed Isabelle where her ruffle had been. "And hers didn't. But they were very much alike, nevertheless.

"And she just raced off. I'm sure I don't know where she's gone to. Very odd, I must say." Aunt Maude shook her head. "The sermon today was very short. I suspect the minister was off to play golf, as I saw he had on plaid trousers under his robe. Why not, on such a splendid day? What's the marvelous smell?"

"That must've been Frannie," Isabelle said. "She's coming for Sunday dinner. Are you staying, Aunt Maude?" Isabelle asked, eyes wide and innocent. She knew perfectly well wild horses couldn't keep Aunt Maude from staying.

"Oh, not today, child. I must hurry home to watch the candidates debate on TV. I must say, they all seem too young, too shifty, always calling each other names," Aunt Maude said. "Very ungentlemanly, if you ask me. It seems to me they set a very bad example for the young people of this country."

"Hello, Maude," said Isabelle's mother. "New hat? Very chic, I must say."

"Do you really like it? I ordered it from the L. L. Bean catalogue," Aunt Maude confided, beaming. "Some boys made noises at me when I came out of church, and when I asked them what they were doing, they said, 'Imitating a duck.' Then they all quacked at me. Well, since this is a duck hunter's hat, I was thrilled. I wear it to the beach too. It keeps the sun out of my eyes. What *is* that divine smell?"

The doorbell rang and Isabelle raced to let Frannie in.

But it was Herbie, standing there, scowling down

at the pad and pencil he was holding.

"I can't fight now, Herb," Isabelle told him. "Frannie's coming for dinner. We're just about to eat."

"I'm doing a survey," Herbie announced, puffing out his chest. "For the *Bee*. What's your favorite cereal?"

"Chex," Isabelle said. Actually she liked Cocoa Puffs best, but her mother refused to buy them.

"What's your favorite, pizza or Chinese?"

"Hey, I thought you were art editor of the *Bee*," Isabelle said. "What's this got to do with art?"

"I'm a man of all jobs, Iz," Herbie said ponderously. "I think I'm slated for the top job. They've got me in training."

Behind him, Isabelle saw Frannie coming up the walk, taking tiny, mincing steps.

"I was unavoidably delayed," Frannie said.

"Sheesh!" said Herbie. "Where'd you find *her*?" and he darted off, shouting, "Catch ya later, Iz!"

"This is my friend Frannie, Aunt Maude," Isabelle said. "She's an . . ."

"Let me," Frannie ordered, shoving Isabelle aside. "I'm a norphan, you see," she told Aunt Maude who, upon hearing these words, put a little hand over her heart and drew down the corners of her mouth as if she might burst out crying. "My old daddy died and . . ." Frannie broke off and said, "What's that smell?"

"Turkey," said Isabelle.

"Turkey!" cried Aunt Maude and Frannie in unison.

Aunt Maude threw up her hands and cried, "Gorgeous!"

And Frannie said softly, "It's not even Thanksgiving or Christmas."

Isabelle's father appeared, whipping off his apron and calling, "*À table!*"

"That's French for 'Soup's on,'" Isabelle explained as they all trooped into the dining room and stood gazing at the big bird.

"How many pounds, Dad?" Isabelle asked.

"Fifteen and a bit," her father answered. "And my special stuffing will take your breath away. It's got oysters in it, among other things. Please be seated, ladies and gents. Maude, you here, and Frannie, here," and he pulled out chairs for them.

"Oysters," Frannie whispered, turning pale. "Inside him?" and she pointed at the turkey with her elbow. Philip grinned at her and said, 'Yeah, they're swimming upstream too," which made Frannie even paler.

"Oysters don't swim upstream," Isabelle scoffed. "Don't pay any attention to him, Frannie. That's salmon who do that. I saw it on TV. My father's stuffing is the best."

"Ahhh, now comes the moment of truth," Isabelle's father said, brandishing his knife, preparing to dissect the turkey. Frannie's eyes were riveted on him as he began to carve. She watched, fascinated, as the slices fell away.

"As you can see," Isabelle said proudly, "my father's an excellent carver."

"Is he a doctor?" Frannie asked, elbows on table, and Isabelle's father stopped carving and a pleased look stole over his face.

"Funny you should ask, Frannie," he said. "My mother always *thought* I would have made an excellent surgeon."

And in her little, tinny voice which carried to the four corners of the room, Frannie said, "When my Aunt Ruth had her operation, she said the doctor carved her up something fierce. She has a scar from her belly button to her armpit, she says. So I just thought you might be a doctor."

The telephone rang just then and they all jumped. Philip leaped to answer.

"You're at dinner, tell her, Philip," Isabelle's father said. "Say you'll call back when we're finished."

Frannie and Isabelle listened as Philip told the caller they were at dinner. It took him quite a while.

"Who was it?" Isabelle wanted to know and Philip looked at her and said, "Wrong number." Frannie giggled and Aunt Maude said, "I'd like a bit of skin, if I may. Skin's my favorite," which sent Philip into such spasms of suppressed laughter he was almost sent from the table.

Isabelle noticed that Frannie patted her mouth daintily after every bite and was impressed. Mouthful of mashed potatoes, pat, pat. Mouthful of turkey, pat,

pat. Dab of cranberry sauce, pat, pat. Frannie left her stuffing alone, Isabelle noticed.

"Perfectly delicious," sighed Aunt Maude contentedly. "I never tasted such turkey in my life."

"After, let's go to your house," Isabelle whispered as she and Frannie and Philip cleared the table.

Frannie scowled and said nothing. "I have to be very careful," she said. "I don't want to spill anything on my frock."

Isabelle went to the bathroom and spent some time jiggling the handle to make the toilet stop running. By the time she emerged, Frannie had gone.

"But I was going to go see where she lived," Isabelle cried. "She said so. She said she'd show me," although in fact, Frannie had not said anything of the kind.

"That's very bad manners, isn't that what you said?" Isabelle asked her mother. "To eat and run, you said, is bad manners—you told me, and that's what she did. She ate and ran."

"She was very polite," Isabelle's mother said. "She said good-bye and thank you for the delicious dinner."

"So I suppose you said, 'Come again, Frannie,' didn't you?" Isabelle said crossly.

"Of course. Why not?"

"How can I be friends with a person who won't ask me to her house? I ask you, how can I?" Isabelle wanted to know.

"I probably *would* have been a good surgeon, when

you come right down to it," Isabelle's father mused. "Imagine that child noticing my skillful carving. Clever little thing."

And "Sheesh!" said Isabelle, standing on her head, trying to make herself feel better. But, for once, standing on her head didn't do any good. No good at all.

SIXTEEN

"I'm back," the tinny voice said close to Isabelle's ear next day.

"Big deal," Isabelle said. "I didn't notice you were gone. I thought you spent the night in the garage." She was still mad Frannie had skinned out so fast yesterday.

"Why, hello Frannie," said Isabelle's mother.

"She's going to teach me to read," said Frannie, poking a thumb in Isabelle's direction.

"Is that so?" Isabelle's mother looked somewhat astonished.

86

"Yes, it's so. Isn't it?" Frannie asked Isabelle, who decided to play her cards close to her vest and give nothing away.

"How come you changed your mind?" she said. "I don't know if I can now. I'm very busy. I have to write a story for a magazine."

"What about?" Frannie wanted to know.

"Yes, what about?" echoed Isabelle's mother, plopping down in the nearest chair as if she planned a lengthy stay.

Isabelle shrugged, not knowing the answer to this question, among many others.

"My life," she said at last. "My life as a child. I plan to tell about my family and the influence they had on me. I plan to write about my school and my teacher and my friends and my enemies. I plan to show all sides of the picture."

Philip charged in, looking for his newspaper delivery bag.

"I bet you took it," he accused Isabelle. "I left it hanging right there and now it's gone. Either you or the weirdo ripped it off. That's pretty sleazy, if you ask me."

"Look in the downstairs closet, Philip. I saw it there yesterday," said his mother.

They sat listening to Philip look for his bag. "I think that's wonderful, Frannie, that you're learning to read. And also wonderful, Isabelle, that you're helping Frannie," Isabelle's mother said.

Frannie put out one finger and caressed a spotted banana lying in a dish.

"That's a very nice banana," Frannie said.

"Help yourself," Isabelle's mother said, "before it goes over the hill. Plenty more where that came from."

Frannie stripped away the banana skin with care.

"It's just the way I like it," she said, holding the banana away from herself, admiring its contours. "I love the smell of bananas."

"I also plan to write a chapter about my brother," Isabelle said.

Philip returned, newspaper bag hanging limply from his shoulder.

"So you found it, did you?" said his mother.

"Well, it was hidden under a bunch of garbage. Somebody knocked it on the floor and it got covered up by all this garbage." Philip's face was red, whether from exertion or embarrassment it was hard to say. "Today's collection day. I gotta get going."

"Actually," Isabelle spoke dreamily, contemplating the ceiling, "actually I plan to write two chapters about my brother. About how when he's on the telephone talking to girls, he's all sweetsie-pie, and when he's in charge at night when my mother and father go out, he's a monster."

"What's this? What's she talking about?" Philip demanded to know.

"Isabelle, if you and Frannie want to be private, better go up and shut your door. Philip, somebody called Sandra called, said she'd call you later."

"Ooooohhh," Philip groaned. "Sandra's having a BYOR party Friday night. That's probably what she wants, to ask me to it."

"BYOR?"

"Yeah. Bring Your Own Record party. You think Dad will let me borrow some of his golden oldies?"

"Probably not. You know how he is about those records of his."

"Yeah," said Philip dryly. "It's like he likes 'em better'n he likes us."

"Oh, I wouldn't go that far," Isabelle's mother said without conviction.

"Follow me," Isabelle ordered. "If we're gonna do this, we better get going."

She dragged Frannie off to her room. "Sit there," she pointed to a spot, and, to her great surprise, Frannie sat.

"First, the alphabet." She went to the blackboard and wrote a big "A." Here's 'A'. We have 'B'. "And she wrote a big "B."

"Listen," Frannie said crossly, "I want to read. I don't need all this baby stuff. I want to read grown-up stuff. Newspapers, instructions on a box of Bisquick, things like that."

Isabelle had watched Mrs. Esposito and other teachers at work and knew the pointer was an important tool. The weasely little kids sat timid in their desks, looking at the teacher, who sometimes loomed very large in their minds, and every gesture the teacher made with her pointer let them know who was boss. She who held the pointer was boss lady, Isabelle had decided long ago.

Isabelle worked her pointer as if she were conducting an orchestra.

"If you get too bossy, I'm checking out," Frannie said.

"First, spell your name," Isabelle said in a cold voice.

"F-R-A-N-N-I-E," said Frannie.

Isabelle wrote "Frannie" on the blackboard.

"Very good," she said. "Now. Your last name."

"Dunn," said Frannie.

Isabelle wrote, "D-O-N-E."

"That's not the way you spell it," Frannie said with a big smile. And she marched over to the blackboard and wrote, "D-U-N-N."

"Hey, it's your name, not mine, kid," said Isabelle.

"Isn't the teacher supposed to know all the answers?" Frannie asked slyly.

"All right." Isabelle got down to business. "Here's the newspaper. This is our target for today." Isabelle waved her pointer furiously. "Here's a headline. Please read it, Frannie."

The headline said, "U. S. Debt Soars."

"U. S.," Frannie said.

"Very good. Short for United States," Isabelle said.

Frannie gave her a dark look and said, "I know."

"All right. Next."

"Debt," Frannie said, pronouncing the silent "b" in "debt."

"Wrong," Isabelle said. "You don't pronounce the 'b' in that word."

"Why not?" Frannie said.

"I don't know, you just don't."

Her mother knocked and came in. "Here's the book you liked so much when you were small, Isabelle," she said, handing her a beat-up little book. "Maybe Frannie would enjoy it." She went downstairs again.

Isabelle opened the book to page one and said, "Sit here, Frannie. By me. This is an easy one. You sound out the words you don't know and I'll help."

"I don't think you're such a hot reader anyway," Frannie said. "I ask you stuff and you don't know the answers. I think I'll go home."

"Listen." Isabelle shuffled off to Buffalo a couple of times, loosening up. "I'm teaching you to read whether you like it or not. Even if I have to sit on you, I'm teaching you."

But Frannie escaped. Isabelle stood at the window and watched her streak down the street.

"Okay for you," she muttered. "You'll be back. Just wait and see."

SEVENTEEN

"Mrs. Esposito," said Isabelle next morning, "I have a problem."

"Would that I had only one," Mrs. Esposito said. "What is it now?"

"I know this kid, she's eight, and she doesn't know how to read or write, and she wants me to teach her," Isabelle said in a rush. "She doesn't go to school."

"Why doesn't she go to school?" Mrs. Esposito asked.

"She's an orphan and they move around a lot, which is why she doesn't," Isabelle explained. "Her mother's out looking for a new daddy on account of the old one died."

Mrs. Esposito scratched her head. "Where do you find your characters, Isabelle?" she said. "Last time it was a goody-goody whom everyone teased. Now this. What next?"

"This kid's smart, but she can't read, and it makes her feel really bad. So yesterday I tried to teach her. It's very aggravating, being a teacher, isn't it?"

Mrs. Esposito smiled and tapped her pencil against her teeth.

"Sometimes," she said. "And sometimes it's very rewarding. My advice would be to get your friend to enroll in school even if she's going to be here a short time. It's against the law for a child's parents to keep him or her out of school. Did you know that? If the authorities found out, they'd insist she go to school."

"Oh, boy," Isabelle said. She never should've told Mrs. Esposito about Frannie. "I didn't know it was against the law," she said.

"Perhaps you could persuade your friend's guardian, or whoever takes care of her, to bring her here. Or, if you like, give me her name and address and I'll see what I can do," Mrs. Esposito said.

"I don't know where she lives," said Isabelle, which was true. "I don't even know her last name. She lives with her aunt, only it's not her real aunt. She might go to school in Michigan. Her mother's horoscope says it's time for a change in her life-style, and she figures Michigan's it."

"Isabelle." Mrs. Esposito bit her lip. "This is absurd. The child should be in school, being taught by a qualified teacher, not a fifth grader."

"It's okay," Isabelle said. "I kind of like teaching her. But I'll tell her what you said."

"If you like, send your friend to see me," Mrs. Esposito said. "Maybe we can work something out without a lot of fuss."

"Okay. I'll tell her. Hey, Herb! Where you been?" Isabelle bopped Herbie on the head with her arithmetic book. "I thought you were sick. How about we fight today after school? After I give Frannie her reading lesson, that is."

"Knock it off," Herbie growled. "I got no time for fighting. I'm depressed."

"Sometimes it helps to talk things over with a friend," Isabelle said in imitation of Mrs. Stern. "What's wrong, Herb? You can unload your problems on me," and she laid a friendly arm around Herbie. He leaped in the air as if he'd been stung by a bee.

"Buzz off!" he cried.

Isabelle grabbed hold of his shoulder in that little place where a pinch can bring a person to his knees. Philip was always grabbing Isabelle in just such a place, and she knew the results well.

"Spit it out," Isabelle said.

Herbie struggled in vain to break her hold.

"Isabelle, enough." Mrs. Esposito's face said she'd had it. Isabelle let go and Herbie shook himself like a dog coming out of the water.

"Sheesh, Isabelle," he said, "you're some tough kahuna."

Isabelle folded her hands and lined up her Adidas and smiled demurely. "I'm known as a very sensible person," she said.

"Since when?" Herbie sneered. "Who says?"

"Mrs. Stern, that's who," Isabelle replied.

"What she know, an old lady like that?"

"Plenty. She's very smart and you know it. Besides, old people know more than young people because they've been around longer."

"Tell it to the Marines," Herbie snorted.

Behind Mrs. Esposito's back, Isabelle made another grab for Herbie. In retaliation, he bit her on the hand.

"If it gets infected, I might have to have a rabies shot!" Isabelle howled.

Herbie leaned close to get a good look.

"I didn't even break the skin," he said. "Too bad my teeth aren't sharper. Besides, you wouldn't get a rabies shot, dumbhead. You'd get a tetanus shot." Herbie was an authority on shots. His mother was on the nervous side, and whenever Herbie so much as looked a little green around the gills, she dragged him to the doctor. Herbie said if there was one thing he didn't want to be when he grew up it was a doctor.

"All those little squirts being dragged into the office

when they get their head caught in a swinging door," he said darkly. "Who needs it?"

The bell rang at that instant. Mrs. Esposito said, "Class, come to order. Everyone sit in his or her seat. I'll warn you now, I've had a tough day and won't put up with any more nonsense."

Mary Eliza Shook waved her hand, wanting to be heard.

"Yes, Mary Eliza," Mrs. Esposito said wearily.

"But, Mrs. Esposito," said Mary Eliza, "this is morning. The day is still in front of us all. We've got a long way to go."

"You're telling me," said Mrs. Esposito.

EIGHTEEN

Next morning when Isabelle got to school, a burly young-
gish man was sitting on the edge of Mrs. Esposito's
desk, swinging his leg, acting completely at home there.

"Where's Mrs. Esposito?" Isabelle asked.

"Not here, that's for sure," he said, grinning at her.
"No, seriously, she's out sick. I'm the substitute."

"We never had a man substitute before," Isabelle
said, looking him over.

"Yeah, I'm one of a kind," he said.

Isabelle sat down at her desk and checked him out.

She noticed the part in his hair started about an inch up from his left ear and his hair went up and over his scalp to the other ear in carefully arranged strands. Idly, she wondered what would happen if he got caught in a high wind.

The only substitute teachers they'd had before were women who wore big black shoes and walked slowly and looked as if they might burst out crying at the drop of a hat. The class usually got totally out of control when one of these substitutes showed up. They raced around the room, throwing things and shouting until the substitute often did burst out crying. Isabelle always felt bad when that happened, even though she'd contributed in large part to the general mayhem.

This guy was different, though. He knew what was what. There'd be no nonsense with him in charge.

That's what he told them. When the bell rang and everyone was seated, he introduced himself.

"Ray Rooney here," he said. "I'm not so long outa fifth grade myself, kids, so no nonsense, okay? I know my way around. I know a substitute means you guys take off and do your thing. Not today, kids. That's not what I'm here for, right? I'm here to give you guys the word on English, arithmetic, social studies, you name it." He got up from the desk and strolled up and down the aisles.

"I've got this terrific memory," he said. "Once I see a face, I never forget that face." He stared hard at

Isabelle, who wriggled in her seat. "Also," he said, "I never forget a person's name. Okay, now I'm going to listen to your names when you call 'em out. Starting with the first row, working backwards, I want you to shout out your name when I point to you. Let's start with you," and he pointed to Mary Eliza Shook.

Mary Eliza stood up and gave a half curtsey and said, "I'm Mary Eliza Shook. I take ballet lessons and I'm going to be eleven next month."

"Good for you. Quiet down, class. Okay, next. Let's go, gang, and no more flap from you, okay, or I might have to get tough."

They loved him. He was the best. They loved Mrs. Esposito too, but she was out sick and she also followed a strict time schedule and didn't keep getting sidetracked the way Ray Rooney did.

"Okay, very good." After roll call Ray Rooney returned to the front of the room and again perched on Mrs. Esposito's desk.

"You're probably wondering where I got this wonky knee," he said in a conversational tone. The whole class fell silent and watched in amazement as the substitute teacher pulled up his trouser leg and showed them his scars.

"Hockey goalie," he informed them, showing where the surgeon had to take out some cartilage. "First team. As a matter of fact, it was first team all the way where I'm concerned. Basketball, football, soccer, lacrosse, you name it. First team."

From the back of the room, a hoarse voice called out, "How about sewing class?" and the room erupted into wild laughter.

"There you go," he said, chuckling.

But not for long. In a flash his face assumed a serious look, and he said, "Never underestimate the value of an education, kids. You guys have got to work hard for your education and your parents have to foot the bill, which means they have to work hard, too. I went to college on a full athletic scholarship. State university, the best there is. I waited on tables, got my lifeguard certificate, pulled a couple people out of the lake, saved 'em from drowning, met a lot of pretty girls. You want to meet pretty girls, men, you better be a lifeguard." He winked hugely. "Lifeguards have lots of muscle, plenty of white teeth, and they attract pretty girls like honey does flies."

He had the class in the palm of his hand.

"Read lots," Ray Rooney told them. "Reading opens doors to the mind. Read everything you can get your mitts on. Without the power to read, you're lost.

"When I was first out of college, I joined the army. Not a bad way to see the world. I went to Alaska, Hawaii, Germany. The whole works. Never paid a cent for my transportation, either. The U.S. government picked up the tab. Join the army and see the world."

Isabelle stole a look at the clock. It was almost time for recess. They hadn't had arithmetic or social studies, never mind English. Mrs. Esposito would have a conniption fit. Isabelle almost hoped Ray Rooney would be back tomorrow, although she didn't want Mrs. Esposito to be *that* sick.

"The thing about reading is, it moves you along," he went on. "You've got to get ready to move right along in this life, and that's what reading does, it moves you along."

Then the loudspeaker crackled, and the principal's voice said, "Attention, please. Will all staff members of the *Bee* please report to my office for an important meeting right after last bell? Repeat: All staff members of the *Bee* please report to my office right after final bell, please."

Then the principal cleared his throat noisily and said, "That is all."

Chauncey cried out, "Hear, hear!" and Herbie hit himself on the head and shouted, "Criminy!" Mary Eliza Shook shot dirty looks at Herbie and Chauncey, and Isabelle could see her lift her behind up and get ready to be first out of her seat. Try to keep Mary Eliza from going to that important meeting of *Bee* staff members. Just try.

"Okay, boys and girls. I guess that about does it for the morning." Ray Rooney looked at the clock. "This afternoon we'll cover anything we missed this morning."

Isabelle felt something move inside her sock. She rolled it down and found a spider resting there. Probably it was a black widow spider. Gingerly Isabelle lifted it out and tucked it neatly into an envelope she happened to have handy. Then she crept up in back of Mary Eliza Shook and shook out the spider from the envelope and down Mary Eliza's shirt.

"Oh, Isabelle," Mary Eliza cooed, "too bad you're not a staff member of the *Bee* so you can go to the meeting this aft." Mary Eliza liked to say "aft" for "afternoon." "I guess we'll decide on our policy. I have all sorts of new ideas I plan to introduce to the board members."

Isabelle smiled and nodded, waiting for Mary Eliza to get the full effect of a spider crawling around inside her clothes. She stood quietly as long as she could. Nothing happened. Life is full of disappointments, Isabelle thought as she ran, gathering speed, out to the playground.

"Slow down!" a sixth grade traffic cop yelled at her. Those traffic cops thought they were such hot shots, Isabelle thought, slowing down, but only a little. Next year when she was in sixth grade, she planned on being a traffic cop. In order to qualify, you had to be responsible and sensible and able to respond in an emergency. She was capable of all those things. She knew she was. Or would be.

If there was one thing she wanted, it was to be a

traffic cop. They were the big shots in the school. She'd rather be a traffic cop than a cheerleader.

Or even a lifeguard.

NINETEEN

"Sound it out, sound it out!" Isabelle yelled.

"I'm bored with sounding it out," Frannie said. And she raised her fragile wrist to her mouth as she'd done that other time, the time she'd cried.

"Don't," Isabelle said, clapping her hands over her ears. "Please don't. I can't stand it if you make that noise again."

Frannie looked surprised. "I'm not making any noise," she said. "I'm smelling my skin. It smells very sweet. How about yours?"

Isabelle beat the eraser against the blackboard, raising a cloud of chalk dust. She'd never known anyone who went around smelling herself. Weird.

"How's it going, girls?" Isabelle's mother asked, sticking in her head to see how they were getting along.

One look at their woebegone, weary faces made her say, "How about coming along to the kitchen? I've got a treat for you. Then maybe you could go to the library. If you haven't been there, Frannie, I bet you'd love it. It's full of wonderful books."

"Okay," Frannie said promptly. "Let's."

Isabelle popped her eyes at her mother and said, "What kind of a treat?" It wasn't Christmas or her birthday or the Fourth of July. Those were treat days. Isabelle's mother didn't buy treats on ordinary days. Only on special occasions.

"It's a surprise," her mother said.

The treat was chocolate-covered ice cream bars on a stick.

"All right!" Isabelle said, taking one, handing one to Frannie. "How come? I thought you said they were too expensive, Mom. That they'd spoil our appetites."

"They were on special," Isabelle's mother said, smiling weakly.

"Don't tell Philip, okay, Mom? If you do, he'll pig out and there won't be any left for me," Isabelle said.

"Oh, I've had these before," Frannie said, slowly peeling off the wrapper. "They're very delicious." She laid her tongue against the cold chocolate and her eyelids fluttered, as if she were waking from a deep sleep. "Very, very delicious."

"Thanks, Mom," Isabelle said in a loud voice. Frannie kept licking and smiling. Isabelle gave her the elbow. "Say, 'Thanks,' " she directed.

"You didn't have to tell me," Frannie said. "I know to say it. Thank you."

Isabelle finished her ice cream before they got to the corner.

"Give us a bite," she said, putting her head next to Frannie's. "Come on, share it. My mother gave it to you, after all," she said and was instantly ashamed of herself. Frannie continued to lick, slowly, silently, savoring every minute.

"You're the greediest kid I ever saw," Isabelle said.

"I can't help it," said Frannie. "Food makes me feel good. When I feel sad and I eat something sweet, I don't feel sad so much."

Isabelle thought about that and felt more ashamed than ever. "When we get to the library," she said, "we walk the wall. It's a rule. We always walk the wall." Frannie said nothing, just kept on licking.

A sign on the library lawn said, "KEEP OFF."

"See? This is it," and Isabelle climbed the low stone wall surrounding the library's green lawn. She stretched out her arms and, putting one foot in front of the other very carefully, she prepared for her tightrope act. It was very dangerous; death defying, in fact. One false step meant curtains. Her heart ticked in her

106

throat as she leaned for a look at the crowds massed below, making bets on whether she'd make it. After she returned to earth, victorious, the news media would then bombard her with requests for interviews, talk shows, maybe even make an offer in six figures for exclusive rights to the story of her life.

Isabelle took a deep breath of the cold, thin air, filling her lungs with oxygen to keep herself going. It was like being on a mountaintop when you were up this high, Isabelle decided. Frannie was behind her, but she was leading the way. "Keep going!" she shouted, giving Frannie encouragement.

"Hey!" Isabelle shouted, enraged to see Frannie skinning down the steps of the children's room. "Hey, wait up!" and Isabelle fell off her tightrope and skinned her knee. But Frannie didn't pause.

"Oh, yes," Frannie was saying when Isabelle made it inside, "I read all the time. I read lots of books. I'm a norphan, you see, and I live alone. I don't even have a dog."

Isabelle watched the librarian's face crumble.

"Oh, you poor child," she said.

To make matters worse, Becca was standing at the desk, with a huge pile of books ready to check out.

"Hello, Isabelle," Becca said. "What are you doing here? I thought you didn't like to read." Becca was Guy's sister, Becca of the paper chains made for every book she read, Becca, the gifted and talented, the piano player, the six-year-old know-it-all.

The last person in the world Isabelle wanted to see right this minute.

"Oh," Isabelle said, bending the truth a touch, "I come to the library all the time."

"She says I can have a library card as I can write my name," Frannie told Isabelle. "This is Isabelle," Frannie introduced Isabelle to the librarian.

"Yes," Ms. Totten said, smiling a welcome, "I know Isabelle."

"Who's that girl?" Becca said.

"Frannie. She's an orphan," Isabelle said. It was the only thing she could think of to say.

Becca marched up to Frannie and said, "I'm Becca. I'm six. I've read fifty-nine books. How many have you read?"

Frannie's tongue touched her upper lip, and she said, "I've lost count."

"Do you go to our school? How come I've never seen you?" Becca asked.

"I'm only visiting," said Frannie.

"Want to come over to my house? Want to see my chains?" Becca said.

The thing that killed Isabelle was, Frannie didn't even say, "What chains?" All she said was, "Sure. Let's go."

TWENTY

"*My mother says you can sleep over Friday night,*
Jane," Isabelle said.

"I can't," Jane Malone said, ducking her head and
hiding behind her hair. Jane was still shy, even though
she and Isabelle had been friends for a while.

"How come?" Isabelle asked. "I been grounded, and
now I'm not anymore, and I dearly want you to come
sleep over at my house. Please, Jane, please please
please," and Isabelle rocked and rolled on the playground to show Jane how very much she wanted her
to sleep over.

"I told Mary Eliza Shook I'd sleep over at her house, that's why," Jane said.

"Mary Eliza Shook thinks she's the greatest thing since sliced bread!" Isabelle hollered. "Tell her you have a virus or a toothache or something. We're watching *Sound of Music*, and my father's making popcorn with real butter. Please, Jane, please please please."

"I can't, Isabelle. I promised Mary Eliza," Jane said. "Next time I'll come to your house and bring my telescope so we can look at the planets. I love to look at the planets." Jane was good in science. She could name all the major planets. Isabelle could name all the seven dwarfs, and Mary Eliza Shook could name all thirteen of the original colonies. It depended on what you were interested in, Isabelle decided.

"I never saw a planet, I don't think," Isabelle said.

"Well, my uncle gave me a telescope just because he knew I wanted one," Jane said, "and it's a very good one. You can see all kinds of wonderful things in the heavens. I saw *Sound of Music* about eight times. I liked it," Jane said, "but I like scary movies better."

"You do?" Isabelle was amazed. Jane didn't seem like the kind of person who'd like scary movies. She was so quiet and shy. Scary movies scared Isabelle. Every time she came home from one, Philip chose that moment to hide in the dark at the top of the stairs and pounce out at her, waving his arms and shouting. That scared her more than anything else. She didn't let Philip know, but somehow he seemed to anyway.

"The best thing is to look at a scary movie through a straw hat," Jane said. Jane came up with lots of surprising ideas, Isabelle thought.

"I have a hat I found in the lost and found," Isabelle told Jane. "It's red and it has a lovely floppy brim. Could I watch scary movies through it, do you think?"

"No," said Jane firmly. "It has to be a straw hat."

"Why?" Isabelle wanted to know.

"Because of the holes," Jane said. "Straw hats have tiny holes in them and if the movie gets really weird, with slimy green creatures coming through the walls dripping blood and stuff like that, oozing all over everything, well, you just hold your straw hat to your face—over your eyes, that is—and look out through the holes so you only see a little bit, not the whole thing, and it's not so bad. Try it sometime."

"Can I borrow yours?" Isabelle asked.

"Sure," said Jane. "If I'm not using it. Or if we went to the movie together, we could take turns."

That Jane, Isabelle thought on her way home. She was a peach of a person. Even if she had won the fifty-yard dash that Isabelle planned on winning on field day, Jane was a star. Sally Smith was a star too, but in a more flaming way. Jane was a quietly burning star whose light was very dependable. If Jane promised to write to somebody, she'd do it. Not like Sally Smith, who didn't keep her promises.

Her mother had left a note to call Mrs. Stern. "Party

111

on Sunday." Her mother's handwriting was like chicken tracks, Isabelle thought. "Old clothes. Let know how many."

Isabelle went over to Herbie to tell him about the party and also to fight. They hadn't fought for a while, and she was ready. When Herbie came to the door, he looked befuddled, as if he'd just gotten up from a nap.

"Mrs. Stern's having a party Sunday, and you're invited, Herb," she said.

"Can't make it," Herbie said. "I'm all tied up."

"What's with you, twerp? I said 'party.' Eats and stuff."

"I'm an executive now," Herbie informed her. "I've got responsibilities. Times have changed, Iz. As art editor of the *Bee*, I'm a big wheel."

"Now I've heard everything," Isabelle said, rolling her eyes. "I thought you wanted out of the job. You said you didn't even know what an art editor does, and now you're all gung ho. You sure do change your mind fast, Herb."

"Yeah, I'm power hungry now," Herbie said, hitching up his trousers. "Chauncey and them tried a hostile takeover and I outfoxed 'em, so now I've got the job. When the principal called a staff meeting, he asked me for my advice. That kinda gets to you, Iz. Until you've been through it, you wouldn't understand."

"I don't believe you," said Isabelle.

"I'm the boss," Herbie told her, a slow smile filling

his face and lighting up his ever-present orange-juice mustache. "I'm on a power trip, Iz. Try to understand."

"First thing you know, you'll be wearing a three-piece suit," Isabelle said scornfully. "With a vest."

"Never!" Herbie vowed, horrorstruck at the thought.

"And if you foul up, Herb, you'll be out on your ear. That's when you find out who your real friends are," Isabelle said, shaking her head.

"My mother's flipping," Herbie said. "She calls me 'My son, the art editor.' It's kind of nice having your mother look up to you, Iz."

"Well, I guess that puts the kibosh on you and me fighting every day," Isabelle said. "You being all tied up with the bigwigs."

"I'll always have time for you, Iz, you know that."

"How about right now?" and Isabelle put up her dukes.

Herbie checked his watch.

"No can do," he said. "I'm late for a meeting right now," and he opened the door and zoomed past Isabelle, almost knocking her down. She put out a foot, hoping to trip him, but Herbie was long gone.

TWENTY-ONE

"We're going out for dinner, Isabelle," her mother said. "And Philip's going to a party. Mrs. Osborn's coming to sit. And, Isabelle"—her mother lifted Isabelle's chin so they were looking directly into each other's eyes— "I know I don't have to tell you no mask, no flippers, no skin diving while we're gone."

"Mom!" Isabelle was shocked. "Of course not."

"Please repeat after me, 'I will not use my mask or flippers in the bathtub. I will not skin-dive in the bathtub.' "

Isabelle solemnly repeated what her mother had said, word for word.

"Amen," said Isabelle's father.

Isabelle and Mrs. Osborn got along fine. Mrs. Osborn spent her days watching the soaps and knitting. When Isabelle's parents had gone, Mrs. Osborn filled Isabelle in on what had happened since they'd last met.

Marylou, it seemed, had had a miscarriage, and Teddy's girlfriend was killed in a car crash, and Nicole signed a million-dollar modeling contract with a no-good advertising genius. "I never trust the ones with the gold chains, Isabelle," Mrs. Osborn said. "They're no good, each and every one. No man worth his salt would wear a gold chain around his neck with his chest hair sticking out, and that's all I'll say on the matter."

Then Mrs. Osborn's daughter called her up to chat, and Isabelle watched a program about health spas. The people who went there ate special food, drank special water, did special exercises, and took baths made of special mud. All of this cost a mint, of course, but it was worth it.

Isabelle watched, fascinated, as a woman was coated with mud from head to toe. She wore a towel wrapped around her head; otherwise she was mud.

"Delicious," the woman kept saying, "perfectly delicious," as if she were eating the stuff. "A mud bath makes me vibrant, desirable," she went on. "My skin feels so soft and smooth when I'm through, it's like a newborn baby's. A mud bath makes me look twenty years younger. I feel reborn. I feel beautiful, and I *am* beautiful."

"Well, you look pretty funny to me, toots," Isabelle told the woman.

But why not? Isabelle asked herself. Why the heck not?

So, as Mrs. Osborn chatted up a storm, Isabelle went out to the backyard and filled a bucket with dirt from her father's garden. He'd never miss it. There was plenty more. It was nice clean dirt, smelling of the earth, which, when you came right down to it, it was. She brought the bucket full of dirt inside and slowly added water to it, careful not to make it too thick or too thin. When she'd got it just right, she lugged the mud up to the bathroom, closed the tub drain, took off her clothes, and dumped the mud into the tub. Then she put on her mother's plastic shower cap and climbed in, careful not to skid.

"Aaaaahhhh," sighed Isabelle, lying full-length so the mud would cover her completely. She could've used another bucketful, she thought, but it was too late for that. "Aaaaaahhhh, yes, but this is delicious," she said, patting herself on the cheek and under her chin, as the woman had done on TV. "Like a baby's behind, it's so smooth. And just as messy." That made her laugh so hard she swallowed some mud. It didn't taste bad. Not something you'd order if you went out to a restaurant, but not bad at all.

She closed her eyes and lay there, feeling her skin getting purer, more beautiful with every passing moment. How vibrant she would be, how desirable. Too bad she didn't have a camera. How long was she supposed to lie there anyway? Half an hour should do it.

"Isabelle!" Mrs. Osborn tapped on the bathroom door. "Are you all right, dear?"

"Super!" Isabelle shouted.

"Well, your father's home. He came after his eyeglasses," Mrs. Osborn said, "and when I said I thought you were in the bathroom, he said, 'Oh, Lord, better go see what she's up to,' and here I am."

"Isabelle." It was her father speaking. "You in there?"

"Yes, Dad," Isabelle said.

"You're not up to any mischief, are you?" he asked. "Anything wrong?" His voice sounded so anxious she said, to reassure him, "I'm taking a mud bath is all."

A silence, thick as the mud that bathed her, filled her ears. Then her father said, quite calm, quite cheerful, considering, "You're what?"

"Taking a mud bath," Isabelle said. "They showed it on TV. You put mud in the tub, then you get in. It's very good for you. It's ..."

She saw the doorknob turn, ever so slowly. She hadn't locked the door; as long as Philip wasn't home there was no need.

"Hi, Dad," she said, waving as her father's face appeared, cautiously, around the edge of the door. "Hi," and she waved, scattering mud all over.

Her father opened and closed his mouth without saying a word. His head waggled back and forth, back and forth, as if he couldn't believe what he was seeing.

"How do you like me?" Isabelle said. "Pretty funny looking, huh? When I'm finished I'll look twenty years younger too. When I wash it all off."

"Isabelle," he whispered in a hoarse voice, "I'm going to close this door, Isabelle, get my glasses and go back to the Warrens'. I'm going to have a nice dinner. I'm not saying a word of this to your mother. I wouldn't want to spoil her evening. We'll discuss it in the morning. Good night."

What'd I do this time? Isabelle wondered. I didn't get the floor wet, I didn't break my promise not to use mask or flippers. I didn't skin-dive. What the heck was he so uptight about, anyway?

TWENTY-TWO

Isabelle scrubbed the bathroom until her arms gave out. Her mother stood at the bathroom door, arms folded, supervising the cleanup job.

"Health spa, indeed," her mother muttered.

"Can I go now, Mom?" Isabelle said at last. "I'll be late for the party."

"Not before I run a final check," her mother said, peering into the corners, peering into Isabelle's ears. "That old gag about being able to grow potatoes in your ears applies here," she said. "How about your hair? Did you wash it?"

"Can't you tell?" Isabelle said.

"Okay, you can go now. But, Isabelle"—her mother held her by the shoulder, preventing her from skinning out—"next time you get a marvelous idea, ask me first. If I could anticipate some of your wild and wonderful plans, I'd be ahead of the game. But, as it is, it's sort of frightening. What goes on inside your head, I mean. I never know what you're going to come up with next."

"Me either," said Isabelle. "It's really weirdsville."

"You're telling me," her mother said, with feeling.

"Tell Frannie, if she comes, to go over to Mrs. Stern's house," Isabelle said. "Tell her I couldn't call her up because I don't know her telephone number. Tell her . . ."

"Get going." Her mother patted Isabelle's rear end. "If Frannie shows up, I'll run her over."

"How do you like this shade?" Mrs. Stern said, holding up a paintbrush. Isabelle was glad to see Mrs. Stern had on her old "CAPE COD" T-shirt and paint-spattered jeans. She liked her better that way, she decided.

"It's kind of phewey, if you ask me," Isabelle said. "What color is it?"

"Plum," said Mrs. Stern. "Maybe a touch of blue.

Yes, that's better. And perhaps a spot of white, and a touch of scarlet. I *do* like scarlet, don't you? There. What do you think, Isabelle?"

"It's better."

"Let's slap some on to get the effect," Mrs. Stern said, handing Isabelle a paintbrush.

That was the part Isabelle liked, slapping on the paint.

"Oh, yes, I like that," Mrs. Stern said, standing back to study the job. "Very nice, Isabelle." She narrowed her eyes. "Very nice indeed."

"Did John go yet?" Isabelle asked, as if she'd just realized John wasn't there.

"Yes, he left two days ago," Mrs. Stern said.

"Is he coming back?"

"Oh, yes, he'll come back to visit me." Mrs. Stern slapped some plum on. "I told him no, Isabelle. I told him I was flattered at being asked for my hand, but I didn't think I wanted to marry again at this late date, that I was quite content as I was and I found him wonderful company and hoped we'd still be friends. And he said we would be, always.

"Yes, that's a very nice warm color," she said. "I thought you'd want to know," Mrs. Stern said. Isabelle nodded, and they painted away in a companionable silence.

"I'm glad you're not going to Florida," Isabelle said at last.

"Me too," said Mrs. Stern.

Then Herbie and Guy showed up, with Frannie not far behind.

"I went over to Herbie's house," Guy said, "and he said Mrs. Stern was having a party so here I am."

"And very welcome you are too, Guy," Mrs. Stern said. "Here, slap a little paint on and be careful with the spattering. I hate a messy painter."

"If you need any worms, Mrs. Stern," Guy said, painting as if he were walking on eggs, "me and Bernie are in the business. We guarantee our worms. They're the best worms in the world."

"Oh, that's good to know, Guy. I could certainly use some for the garden. They make the flowers grow better, I understand," Mrs. Stern said.

"This is Frannie." Isabelle introduced Frannie to Guy. "She's an orphan."

"I was over at your house," Frannie told Guy. "I saw Becca's chains. They're not so much. I'm going to make my own chains when I go to Michigan."

"Oh, Frannie dear, I didn't know you were going to Michigan," Mrs. Stern said.

"My mother's coming for me soon," Frannie said. "She said she was coming for me very soon."

After they finished painting the hall, they all trooped into the kitchen for refreshments.

"This is indeed a joyous occasion," Mrs. Stern said, smiling around at them all. "Good friends gathered together is my idea of a real party, a real celebration. I'm so glad you're here."

"We're glad we're here too," said Isabelle, eyeing the plate of Oreos, and Frannie patted the bowl of fruit in the center of the table and said, "That's a very lovely banana."

TWENTY-THREE

"Mrs. Stern's boyfriend John asked her for her hand in marriage, but she decided not to give it to him," Isabelle told her mother and father next morning at breakfast. She sprinkled brown sugar on her cereal.

"She didn't want to go to Florida to live, she said. There are too many old people there, you see. Plus, John wanted her to live in his condo where she wouldn't have to lift a finger. She likes to lift her fingers so she's not going, she's staying here."

Isabelle's father finished eating his egg, wiped his

mouth, and said, "I'm glad to hear that, Isabelle. Now." He patted his pockets, checking for his wallet. "A word to the wise is sufficient, I believe. Listen carefully, Isabelle."

"Yes, Dad," Isabelle said meekly.

"No more mud baths. That is an order. I'm not asking, I'm telling."

"Yes, Dad," Isabelle said again.

"Of course, I'd feel safer if you stayed out of the bathroom entirely," he said. "If there were some way I could work it out, I would. One way or another, you're bad news in the bathroom, Isabelle."

Isabelle nodded, enjoying the crunchy sound of the cereal between her teeth.

"I've been thinking, Dad," she said.

"Of what?" her father said, looking alarmed. "What now?"

"Well," she said, "how about an outhouse? You could build one in the backyard. Wouldn't that be kind of neat?"

Isabelle's father pushed back his chair and rose hastily.

"Got a tough day coming up, dear," he told Isabelle's mother. "I'll probably be late tonight. Don't wait supper for me." He kissed his wife and daughter.

"Do me a favor, Isabelle," he said. "Go out and climb a couple trees, why don't you? Dig a ditch, run a few miles. But don't get any more bright ideas, all right?"

125

"Sure, Dad," Isabelle said, thinking fathers sometimes acted very weird, very strange.

"It must be tough, being a father," Isabelle said after her father had gone. "Having to go to work every day to earn money. Dad must get tired of it sometimes. Maybe he needs a vacation."

"Nothing wrong with Dad that time won't cure," her mother said. "Once you and Philip are out of college and off on your own, he'll be a new man. When that happens, we'll go off on our own, too. Maybe go on safari in Africa or go around the world, on a tramp steamer or something."

"Hey, neat!" Isabelle cried. "Can I come too?"

Summer lingered, spinning out its lazy days, drawing the children into its web as surely as any spider, lulling them into a false sense of permanence, giving the illusion it was here to stay.

Then, one morning in early September, Isabelle went out to the yard, barefoot, as usual. The dew on the grass was *cold*. "I mean, cold," Isabelle grumbled, going back in to put on her new droopy socks and her Adidas.

"Just when you think summer's forever," she said, "it pulls a fast one."

And where was Frannie? Frannie had disappeared from the face of the earth, or so it seemed.

"Where's your pal, the space cadet?" Philip asked.

"The weird-looking chick? She fall into a well or something? Maybe got gnawed on by a grizzly? Or did she just cut and run, take off, never to be seen or heard from again?"

"Her name's Frannie, for your information," Isabelle said. "And she's not any weirder looking than those dudes who call you up all the time. 'Hello' " Isabelle let her voice go high and whiny, imitating the girls who called Philip. " 'Is Phil there?' Next time one of those totally gnarly dudes calls, I'm telling her you're going to the bathroom and you left strict instructions not to be disturbed. On account of . . ."

Philip's face darkened. "You do and I'll . . . How'd you like to wind up twisting in the wind, toots?" he snarled.

Isabelle shrugged. She'd heard worse threats.

"Maybe she's got a virus," she mused. "Or maybe she broke her leg."

"Maybe she robbed a bank," Philip suggested. "Or went off with the circus. Or there's always the bubonic plague."

"What's that?" Isabelle said. "What kind of plague's that? I never heard of that."

"Well," Philip said slowly, "it's nearly always fatal. Wipes out thousands just like that," and he snapped his fingers. "I know. She's probably doing TV commercials, scarfing down everything in sight and getting paid for it. I can hear her now. 'This cereal will make you the strongest kid in your class.' Chomp, chomp. Or 'Drink Poopsy Cola and win friends.' Or 'Make your sandwiches with Fatty's bread and develop your muscles.'" Philip chortled hugely at his own wit.

"Man, that'd be the life," he sighed. "Eating up a storm and getting paid big bucks for it. Man, oh, man."

But where *was* Frannie?

"If anything had happened to her," Isabelle's mother said soothingly, "we would've heard."

"Who from?" Isabelle demanded. "We don't know where she lived or her telephone number. I don't know her Aunt Ruth's name, even. And she didn't go to school so we can't even check with the principal to find out. There's nobody who would tell us if anything had happened to Frannie."

Then Isabelle stopped worrying and got mad.

"Boy, she has her nerve," she said. "After we were so nice to her and all, she could've at least told us she was going away."

"Such a sad little thing she was," Isabelle's mother said, shaking her head.

"Sad!" Isabelle cried. "She wasn't sad. She was a tough character is what she was. A really tough character. I never knew anybody like her." She thought a minute. "Not even Mary Eliza Shook."

"But she had to be tough, didn't she?" Isabelle's

mother said. "She didn't have much choice."

Once in a while Isabelle's mother astonished her.

"Yeah," she said, mulling over what her mother had said. "Yeah, I guess you're right, Mom. She didn't have much choice."

TWENTY-FOUR

The day before Halloween, a postcard arrived for Isabelle.

"Mail for you, scuz," Philip said, tossing it at her.

"Oh, no," Isabelle said with a big grin. So Sally Smith had kicked through at last. Good ole Sally, she's true-blue, Isabelle told herself. There was a picture of a big moose standing by a very blue lake. It was a beautiful picture and struck Isabelle as very artistic. She turned it over to see what Sally had to say.

But it wasn't from Sally Smith.

The message read:

> *Dear Isbel,*
> *I go to scool now. I can read some.*
> *Your a good teach. Thanx.*
>   *Yr frend, Frannie D.*

"Yippee!" Isabelle shouted. "Hurrah!" And although she was already late for school, she dashed up to her room, and wrote, "ONCE UPON A TIME" in big letters on the blackboard. Then she raced back down. She'd finish the story when she got back.

About the Author

Constance C. Greene has been writing for many years, starting in New York City as a reporter for the Associated Press. In 1969 she began her career as a children's book author and has since written seventeen books for Viking, including *A Girl Called Al* and *Beat the Turtle Drum*, both selected as Notable Books by the American Library Association. She is a leading writer of contemporary fiction for young people.

Mrs. Greene and her husband live on Long Island; they have five grown children.